I MARRIED MY DEAD COUSIN'S HUSBAND

LALA B.

ISBN-13: 9781234567890

ISBN-10: 1477123456

Cover design by: Lala B.

Library of Congress Control Number: 2018675309

Printed in the United States of America

Dedication

To my diary in human form who left me way too soon. I love you
Cuzo and I hope you are resting well. We will turn up again.

Contents

Trigger Warnings

Ok baby love this one is going to be a mild case of crazy, well by my standards, very spicy, filled with explicit language and a mildly violent scene, along with a mention of rape, and explicit sex scenes. Buckle up baby love this is a short but wild ride, I hope you enjoy it.

Prologue

I Married My Dead Cousin's Husband is a scorching second-chance romance tangled in family secrets, forbidden desire, and dark deception. Sapphire Bentley knew marrying Hazekiel "Haze" Perkins would raise eyebrows and unearth buried sins. He was her cousin's husband. Now he's hers. Haze is intense, magnetic, and maddeningly off-limits. Their chemistry is volatile, their connection undeniable but his past with her cousin casts a long, seductive shadow neither of them can escape. As passion explodes and old wounds resurface, Sapphire uncovers shocking truths that could destroy her family. Someone is watching. Someone is digging into what really happened the night her cousin died.

Will they get to live happily ever after, or will all the family secrets ruin their holy matrimony?

Chapter One

Sapphire Bentley

"Ride that shit my cowgirl." He commands and I do just that.

"Fu... fuckkk Haze." I moan and gush all of over his large dick, but I keep bouncing as I feel his orgasm cresting.

"Ma... Ma wake up, ma." Dontrell is trying to shake me awake.

"I'm up. I'm up baby." I try to sit up but notice the wet spot between my legs and stop, holding the blanket at my chest.

"I'm up papa, go get ready for school." I rush him out of the room and get up to change my covers. I can't believe I had the damn dream about Haze again. That man has been plaguing my dreams for months now. I guess its because it has also been heavy on my mind to hit up my god baby and see how she's doing. I moved the kids to Houston, Texas four years back after leaving the kids cheating ass father once and for all. I am still surprised at myself for staying with him for eleven damn years. Malakhi was the best the first few years after he went pro during college then he just turned into the hoe of the west. I went to college for Computer Networking with a minor in cybersecurity, so I started two years ago working for Houston utilities making good money, so much so I recently bought our first home, a four-bedroom, three and half bath, brand new build, with a large yard and pool. The kids have been the happiest I have seen them, but I noticed they were also missing their god sister as much as I was. I got the kids ready and off to school once I got myself together after that wet dream then headed out to work. I've been at work for about four hours now and It's time for lunch, so I grab my belongings to head out. I notice a message notification from my Insta and quickly open the message once I notice it's from Haze. He was such a fine chocolate boy when we were growing up. I always thought we would end up together but somehow while I was away at college he ended up with my cousin. I decided to go looking at his recent pics before responding to his message and he is even finer than he was back then.

Haze: Hi Sapphire, Harmony has been asking about you all and she is growing up so fast. How are you and the kids?

Me: We are doing great even better job, finally a bigger home. I miss my girl so much too. I hate that I let life get so busy.

Haze: She misses you too, we both do.

Me: I'm sorry I was so focused on my girl, I forgot to ask how are you doing?

Haze: I'm doin good just raising our girl and training these knuckleheads on the base since I'm no longer being deployed.

Me: I see you. Well, give my girl my number 770-637-8212. I would love to hear from her.

Haze: Bet I just texted it to her. She's hanging with your aunt.

She texts me right away and we continue to do so throughout the day. I was so happy to see my girl video calling me as I was leaving my office.

"Hi Goddy, I miss you where have you been?" She shouts the moment her pretty face appears on my screen.

"Goddy misses you too babygirl. I apologize for that. I allowed life to get the better of me with the moves and new jobs." I try to explain to her sad face.

"Well, I guess I get that but does this mean you're coming back home?"

"Oh, baby we live in Houston, Texas now but I do plan on visiting and calling more. I'm going to text your number to your siblings, they have been missing you too."

"Really, I miss them too. I can't wait to talk to them. Well do you think you guys can come over for my birthday in two months?" She asks me and I am just glad she's not too mad to invite me for her birthday celebration.

"I will put in my vacation time when I get into the office tomorrow to make sure I am there, I promise. Did your dad already make plans?" I grab my belongings from the peanut butter passenger seat in my white Range Rover to head into the house while still holding the phone in view. I'm not surprised to walk into the house being quiet, the kids are still at martial arts and dance practice. The other perk to my new career is most days I beat my kids home.

"I don't think so but sometimes he likes to surprise me for my bday."

"Ok I will get with him to see what we're doing but baby let Goddy get dinner ready for your sister and brother. You can text me though." I advise her as I'm walking up the stairs to my large master bedroom. I was so shocked when this house

9

became available in my budget. I jumped on it after we walked through just for this room as well as the pool. My room is on the other side of the house from the kids' room, large double doors to enter, I can fit my first apartment in here and still have room, plus the bathroom and walk in closet are everything.

"Ok mommy talk to you later. I love you." When she said those words, I felt so warm and full of joy again.

"I love you too babygirl." I have the biggest smile on my face after talking with her and just like I told her I messaged her dad to see what he was doing for her birthday as well as sent over her number to Destiny and Dontrell. By the time I finish getting my hygiene in order I notice Haze has messaged me back with his number telling me to call him, so I do while I get dinner prepared.

"What's up Haze?" I greet him once he answers, and I place my phone on the counter on speaker.

"Shit Phire just getting in and saw your message. I haven't decided just yet and before you start, I know it's only two months away things have just been hectic lately." He rushes to explain because he knows me to damn well. I still can't understand how he could switch up on me the way he did and marry my damn cousin of all people. We would have secret rendezvous with each other to get away from her. She always wanted to sit between us or interrupt a conversation we were having with each other. We kissed multiple times and even made plans for when he would get deployed while I was in college, but whatever it happened.

"Well, if you're cool with it, I can put something together. Is there something she has been wanting to do?" I walk around my chic farm kitchen placing the spaghetti noodles in the boiling pot then start chopping up the onions and bell peppers.

"She has been wanting to go to Disney, but I haven't figured out the best time to plan it like she wants. Baby girl has become so damn picky." He says exhaustedly and I can hear him moving around then it sounds like the shower turns on. I hate myself for the picture that pops in my mind of a naked Haze.

"Ok I can get that done. Does she want the park in Florida or Cali?"

"Florida cause she also wants to visit Universal."

"Ok don't worry about it, I will get everything planned. Destiny has been wanting to go too and since they're last day of school is that week we can make it one big family trip for her." I put the hamburger meat on then toss in the onions and bell peppers I chopped up in the pot too then season it all up.

"Oh, she's going to love this. Just let me know the cost and I will send it over to you."

"No don't worry about that, I'll manage it."

"You are out of your mind Phire. That trip will cost thousands for all of us to go and don't argue with me. You. Are. Not. Paying for it, do you understand me?" He demands and I hear the finality in his voice, so I decide not to argue with him. He has always given off that dominant and big dick energy and that's exactly why I always picked fights, or exited stage left the moment he got to close to me physically after he married her.

That man use to put my body on fire just by looking at me and Lawd don't let him get close to me.

"OK fine I will let you know the cost of it when I finish putting it all together." I swear I don't remember ever being that quick to agree with any man telling me what to do. We talk for a few more minutes, ending the call once he informs me, he's talking to me while in the shower. I walk over to my wine fridge pulling out a bottle of Moscato then turning on some Jill Scott while I finish up dinner. Before I know it, the kids are walking in the door fussing about something.

"Hey... hey what the hell is going on you two?" I question them as they enter the long foyer hallway. It was built with a formal living room in the front, but I turned that into an office for days I get to work from home.

"Hi ma, Destiny has a crush on one of my friends and she's mad because I told him I'd break every bone in his face if he messed with my little sister." I didn't mean to laugh out loud, but I can picture Dontrell threatening his friend with a straight face. Raising two kids alone was never on my bingo card but it's where I am and these two now that Dontrell has hit thirteen and Destiny hasn't fully reconciled her feelings about us leaving the home we shared with her father they are working on my last damn nerve. I blocked them from all the bullshit he put me through at first, so they never realized just how much of an ass he was until recently.

"Ma tell him to stop. All I said was that the darn boy was cute." Destiny huffs throwing her bookbag down on the floor.

"Why are you even trying to talk to the boys at the middle school anyway little girl you haven't even made it there yet." I turn back to the stove to turn everything off as dinner is done.

"The boys at my school are just too childish and they get on my nerves." She continues to complain to me as if I'm going to have her side on this. She just turned eleven in February, and I swear it is like a boy craze switch went off in her head.

"Destiny, I have told you more than once to calm those lil hormones of yours and keep your eyes in your books, but Trell you can't threaten bodily harm to every person, somebody may actually be able to beat you one day." I begin plating the food and they already know that it is queue for them to go wash their hands then sit down for dinner. Destiny continues to huff and puff as she heads upstairs to her room and Dontrell just walks up like he won a prize. All I can do is shake my head as I ask God for guidance and not strength cause if he gives me strength, I might choke one of their asses. We thankfully get through dinner with less attitude and head our separate ways to our rooms after the kids clean up the kitchen. We have a deal when one of us cooks dinner for us all we rotate who cleans the kitchen afterwards. I lay in my bed with the one person on my mind I wish could stop thinking about and clearly God saw it fit to punish me because my phone dings with a text notification and of course it's him.

Haze: It was really good talking with you again, I miss you, but anyway sweet dreams beautiful.

Me: Good night, Haze.

Is all I could text him back. I know him and my cousin had their problems, but I never pegged him for a slime ball part of me still doesn't.

Chapter Two

Hazekiel "Haze" Jenkins

I can't believe Sapphire is finally back in my life. It took everything in me not to catch a flight to Houston to drag her ass back home with me where she belongs. After Monique died though things were so hectic with Harmony acting out and my deployments back then were long and constant. Taking the promotion to be a trainer and only deployed when needed freed up the time I needed to make sure my daughter was doing good mentally as well as keep tabs on the true love of my life. Now I just need to figure out how in the hell to get her to stop seeing me as her cousins widowed husband. Texting her that I missed her was just a start though, I wanted to say so much more but didn't want to scare or piss her off, she has always been the crazy one of the bunch well besides me. I'm so caught up in my thoughts I barely hear Harmony light knocks on my bedroom door.

"Come in babygirl." I shout through the door and in walks my princess, who is growing into a Queen of her own right. Some would never understand why I continue to claim her as mines when I know biologically, she is not. The moment she was born, when I looked into those heart snatching grey eyes I knew she was my lil girl no matter what. She hops in the bed with me like she does every night before she goes to sleep.

"Daddy did Goddy call you about my birthday yet? I really want to see her." She asks, laying her head on my chest then I wrap my arms around her as I always do and always will, even when she's all grown up.

"Yes, she did and she's planning something very special for you."

"Really what daddy? Tell me... Tell me... Tell meeeee." She jumps from my arms and starts to bounce on the bed like a toddler at her big age, in excitement.

"I can't tell you babygirl it's a surprise. Just know that you will absolutely love it, ok?"

"Ok fine. Well good night daddy, love you." She kisses me on the cheek and hops out the bed as I tell her I love her too. I can't wait for her to see what Phire has planned for her. I try to get off to sleep but to say it was hard is putting it mildly. I am way too anxious about seeing Sapphire again and to think it's not for another two months. I finally fall asleep after deciding she will have to come visit us before that or we will go to her. Waking up that morning I put a plan together on how to convince her to let us fly in for the weekend but my babygirl clearly is quicker than me.

"Daddy... daddy I just got off the phone with Goddy and she said they can come see us this weekend. It took some begging and pouting but it worked. We have to get the house ready." She turns in her seat at our large kitchen island where we eat breakfast most mornings. Since turning fifteen she is even more independent, as well as moody with that whole menstrual thing, but most mornings I come down and she's already made us breakfast. Today she has decided on grits, eggs, and our favorite Georgia sausage.

"Looks good baby girl and how did you convince ya goddy to come over this weekend?" I fix my plate and sit down next to her.

"Well, my sister and brother texted me last night and we all kinda came up with the idea of them coming here. We might've pleaded, guilt tripped and promised to make all A's on our next report card to get her to booking their flights over breakfast just now." I can't do anything but smile and shake my head, but I guess it's better than me packing us up and showing up on her doorstep then I would have to explain how I know her address to begin with.

"OK well Dontrell can go in the spare bedroom since I doubt, he would want to sleep with you girls in your room."

"What about goddy, where will she sleep?" I almost slipped and said in my bed but caught myself and told her she can sleep in my office it has a murphy bed in there. Since it's Tuesday she catches a ride with her best friend Ellie who stays next door while I get ready to head on base. The week flies by and before I know it Friday has rolled around. Harmony and I are heading out to the airport to pick them up since I still have to convince her to stay with us. She actually thought I would let them stay in a bnb, clearly this woman is going to be difficult. Pulling up to the curb where Sapphire and the kids are waiting my damn heart stops for a moment. She has always been beautiful but the past eight years have been amazing to her. She previously relaxed her hair but now it is natural in a big curly afro, she has gained a few pounds but damn she is carrying them well, she has braces now which looks really cute on her, and her style has went from tom boyish to super sexy to classy but sexy since you can't miss those damn curves on her short frame. Once I catch myself, I pop the trunk on the Tahoe. "OMG Goddy you look so beautiful." Harmony says jumping out the truck before I can get out and Sapphire drops her bags to wrap her arms around her in a tight embrace.

"You have gotten so big and so beautiful. Damn you look so much like your mom." She expresses and just stares at her for a few moments then the kids just run and collide with each other in hugs.

"She's right you do look beautiful Sapphire." She smiles, drops her head, and pushes a part of her fro behind her left ear.

"You are looking pretty good yourself Haze. The army has done you good." She's still avoiding eye contact with me, so I step closer lifting her head up by her chin.

"No need to be shy around me woman. I know you all too well and you know how I feel about eye contact." I wish I could just pull her into my arms and plant a kiss on those luscious lips of hers, but I am trying to pace myself.

"Hey kids let's go you can catch up in the car." She turns from me to direct the kids to get into the truck. I grab their suitcases and place them in the trunk. The kids all pile in the backseat together so she sits up front with me. Once she's seated, I reach over to put her seat belt on, close the door, and hop in the truck driving us home. She is looking at me weird and it registers what I just did so I just smile back.

"I forgot to grab some dinner for tonight what do you guys have a taste for?" I question them as it dawns on me that I didn't get to go grocery shopping yesterday.

"Stop by the grocery store I can whip us up something, it's only a little after seven." She says still looking out the window and I'm glad she suggested it because I have missed her cooking greatly. Clearly the cooking gene missed Mo, she couldn't cook for shit.

"Oooh Goddy is cooking this is about to be really good, no offense dad."

"None taken your Goddy can out cook the best of them."

"Oooh ma can you make that crab and steak Cajun pasta you make with that creamy sauce, it's been a while." Destiny asks her from the backseat, and I am thoroughly intrigued by the idea of having this Cajun pasta dish she's requesting. All the kids become in agreement as we pull up to the local grocery store.

"I can't believe this store is still here." Phire says reaching for her door handle to open it, but I stop her by placing my hand on her left arm and looking at her with a raised eyebrow. She knows she has never opened a door around me in the past and neither did Mo, no matter how I felt about her ass, my father raised me old school. I'm not sure why she's playing slow now but I will fix that soon enough. I hop out the truck and walk around to open the door for her as well as the kids and I hold my hand out to help her out the truck, but she hesitates, so I grab her hand gently ushering her out the truck.

"By the way the store is still open because I bought it a few years back when Mr. and Mrs. Brunt's passed away and their kids didn't know how they were going to keep it afloat with the repairs and upgrades it needed. I just couldn't see one of the few Black family owned grocery stores close down. Not too many people know I own it since I left the name and their kids running the day to day as well as they still partially own it." She looks over at me in awe as we walk into the store and grab a cart. We made major upgrades from new registers, carts, better shelving system, partnered with more local farms for produce, meats, and canned goods. Besides my promotion last year to master sergeant this is one my greatest accomplishments and money has nothing to do with it.

"That is really amazing Haze, I hope you're proud of this, I know I am." She finally looks over at me as we're going down the aisles grabbing the ingredients she needs to cook.

"Thanks, I am and that means a lot coming from you." I can tell she's trying to fight her attraction to me just like she used to when Monique was alive but at least this time I'm not getting cursed out every few minutes.

"Hey Mr. Haze can we pick out some fruits. I haven't had any Georgia peaches in a long time." Dontrell asks me rubbing his stomach.

"Of course, come on I'll help you guys pick them out we have some of the best in the county." I leave with the kids heading back to produce and we end up picking out all types of fruits to snack on. The kids split off to check out the snack aisle as I make my way back to Sapphire. I find her in the back near the meat & seafood department but clinch my right fist at the sight of Tremaine Shelton, he was in our junior class while Mo was a sophomore then dropped out before senior year. I stalk over to them trying to control my anger at him grabbing her hand to kiss it like he's some proper gentleman when I know this fool has about four baby mama's running around here right now and one of them crashed a damn car into the last chick house he was involved with.

"There you go Phire the kids and I picked out some great fruit." I announce finally reaching them, then I put my hand on her waist pulling her behind me looking down a bit at Tremaine as my six foot four, two hundred and sixty pound frame is larger than his five ten maybe a buck eighty frame.

"Haze my dude how's it going? I was just telling Sapphire it's been a while since I saw her fine ass." I feel Sapphire staring a hole into the side of my face as I still have her pushed behind me and won't let her move.

"Yea she came back to visit us. How's Jena I heard she just had y'all baby a month ago, what's that six kids now." I look at him and lean my head to the side as he starts to catch my drift of moving his ass along.

"Yea I actually came to grab some stuff for her, I'll catch y'all later. It was good seeing you, Sapphire." He tells her rushing off since I'm sure the look on my face told him how much I wanted to kill his ass for putting his lips on my woman.

"Well, that was rude Haze. What was up with that and before you lie, I can feel the anger radiating off of you."

"Look that nigga ain't shit but a walking STD and you don't need to be anywhere near him. Did you get what you need?" I take a few deep breaths to calm my nerves because I don't want the kids to feel that energy it's bad enough, she did.

"Yea let's go find the kids and I don't need you protecting me from men I'm a grown woman Hazekiel." She walks off clearly mad with me and now I'm kicking myself. This is not how I wanted our first night to go but I know something that may help.

Chapter Three

Sapphire Bentley

I don't know what the hell has gotten into Haze but it's starting to work my nerves but if I'm being honest, it's pissing me off because it's such a fucking turn on and I can't be turned on by this damn man. This weekend is going to be harder than I thought. I finally find the kids in the snack section still debating over what to get and then I notice Haze coming down the aisle from the opposite direction with my favorite bottle of wine, chocolate chip cookie dough, and some pretty multi color roses. I can't help but smile at him even though I am still annoyed with his behavior so far tonight.

"I'm sorry about my attitude earlier Phire." He apologizes as he comes to stand next to me and we walk to the register to check out.

"Just chill out would you." I look up at him and he just nods his head. We get everything checked out and loaded into the truck then take the ride another fifteen minutes to his home and I recognize it immediately as his parents' old home, but he clearly has done a full remodel of the large craftsman style home. We used to spend so many hours on that porch swing just sipping on the homemade lemonade his mom used to make us. I can't believe he kept the swing.

"I know what you're thinking and of course I kept that swing, it was our favorite spot and now it's Harmony's." This man is really laying it on thick and I am truly baffled as to why. He makes us ladies go in the house while him and Dontrell unload the truck then I send the kids to put up our luggage while I put up the groceries I don't need for tonight, but I notice he takes my suitcase upstairs and I just shrug it off for now. I get to chopping up onions, red and green bell peppers that I will need as Haze comes back downstairs then heads for the wine, I put in the fridge grabbing two wine glasses from the cabinet pouring wine in one and handing it to me.

"Hey Alexa play nineties and two thousands soul playlist." India Arie "Brown Skin" starts to play through the speakers, and I'm instantly taken back to the summer before I left for college when we kissed among other things before him and Monique started dating well got married. That night lived rent free in my head for weeks, probably months. I look over to him wondering if he purposely played this song right now but fuck my body is heating up.

"Do you need any help?" He asks coming to stand next to me and I almost cut my damn finger when the chills run down my spine as his arm brushes my shoulder.

"Yea you can take over this and I will start on seasoning the steaks I cut up." I put down the knife to tenderize the steak chunks then season them. I decide to put the wine down because the way my body feels just by the song that is playing, I am in dangerous territory. I start sautéing the steak chunks in the pan while the penne pasta cooks when he comes up behind me with the tray of veggies, he finished cutting up then placing them on the counter next to me as he rests his other hand on my hip.

"That smells amazing Phire."

"Thanks. Can you drain the pasta while I add the crab meat and hand me the heavy cream." I instruct him trying to stay focused on the task at hand welcoming the steam on my face from the hot pan that fogs my glasses. He finally moves to do what I ask him as I take the last piece of steak out the pan then the crab meat before tossing in the veggies letting them cook a bit. I put in a tablespoon of tomato paste, a little beef broth, the heavy cream, some more seasoning, and finally some shredded mozzarella cheese. We get dinner finished up oddly enough working in a comfortable silence but a couple of heated stares that I catch from him when I get lost in a song playing and start swaying my hips. We call the kids down who are upstairs getting caught up with each other and apparently getting in their PJ's. They let us know they are going to have a movie night in Harmony's room after dinner.

"Wow Goddy this is sooooo good." Harmony says excitedly doing a happy dance in her seat.

"This really is good, Phire. I was in here smelling it cook but tasting it is a whole different thing."

"Goddy, I need this at least once a month, pleasssseee."

"You think this version is good you gotta try the one with the sausage and chicken," Dontrell adds in practically done with his food already.

"That can be arranged if you're cool with it, I can bring her there once a month for a weekend." Haze says after chewing up a mouth full of food.

"Wait really, you would bring her to Houston once a month?"

"Sure, I was hoping this was going to be the first of many weekends we all get to hang out together or just her spending time with y'all. As long as that's cool with you."

"Of course it is, you hear that kids once a month we all get to hang out with each other again." The table erupts in cheers and laughter. Soon we're all done with dinner, the kids load up the dishwasher and head upstairs for their movie night but I'm taking my time wiping down the counters. Haze comes back downstairs shirtless showing off his sculpted muscles and all the tattoos covering his dark chocolate skin. That v cut right above his basketball shorts almost make me need a come to Jesus moment with the thoughts of what I would do with my tongue in that area.

"You can use the bathroom in my room to get cleaned up, but we need to talk first, come on." He turns to walk back up the stairs after kissing me on the top of my head and my feet seem to move on their own accord right behind him. Once we make it to his room, he locks the door behind me, and I step in the middle of his large modern African designed master bedroom with my back still facing him because I can't look in those beautiful honey eyes. I feel the moment he gets close before he places his hands on my shoulders rubbing up and down.

"You don't know how many nights I laid awake wishing you would be standing in front of me again." He leans down speaking directly into my ear with his husky deep voice causing goosebumps on my arms and the back of my neck.

"Haze please don't." I start to say as I turn around and the moment I do he presses his soft juicy lips against mines inciting an involuntary moan to escape my throat. He slides his

26

tongue across my lips then pushes his tongue into my mouth. I push him slightly trying to break our kiss.

"Haze we can't do this. You were married to my cousin for God sakes." I breathlessly tell him as he leans his forehead against mines still holding me by my waist.

"Fuck her she has kept us apart long enough baby please stop fighting what I know you've been feeling for just as long as I have." He groans out clearly frustrated but now I'm pissed that he just spoke about my cousin that way, so I push him much harder this time.

"What the hell do you mean fuck my cousin, are you serious right now?" He simply walks off heading towards his walk in closet and rummages a round until he comes out with an envelope that he hands to me then he walks to sit on the edge of his bed.

"What's this Haze?"

"I was hoping you would just give in to the feelings we always had for each other cause I didn't want to taint your view of Monique but clearly you have some false sense of loyalty." I turn to look at him part of me not wanting to know what he meant just by the few things he just said but he continues.

"What's in that envelope is words of a dying woman confessing all her sins. Look, I love you. It's always been you but there is something that is in that letter that may have you looking at me differently as well and I'm fine with that. So, if you absolutely need the truth open and read it or just let me spend the rest of our lives showing you how much I love you." He expresses after standing from the bed walking over to me and caressing my cheek as he peers in my eyes trying to penetrate my heart.

"Haze, I need some time to think about all this. I will admit that I always wondered how you two ended up together after all the time we spent together and if I'm being honest, I was hurt but I knew she didn't know about us so I let it go and figured you played us both." I can't do anything but sigh because this is all too much, and I haven't even read the letter yet.

"Baby I never meant to hurt you never and I was not playing you. It hurt like hell every day to be away from you and be so close sometimes but not be able to touch you, tell you how much you mean to me, ugghhh. Maybe you really should read the letter. I know you and you'd always question us if you don't." He has me so spent with everything he's dropping on me.

"Let's just enjoy this weekend with the kids and maybe we can discuss all this later." I tell him backing away from him, still holding the letter in my hand.

"You can take a few days to think about everything and read that letter but either way I'm coming for you Phire just know that. Now go get washed up." He commands while smacking me on the ass. The rest of our weekend was a blend of laughter, trips to the beach, stolen glances, and brief brushes of our hands or whatever else he decided to rub against me. Today we are headed to the airport and to say the built-up sexual tension in the air is palpable is putting it mildly, I swear you could cut that shit with a knife.

"Goddy do you really have to go?" Harmony questions from the back seat with a pout on her face.

"Yes, babygirl you will be with me in a week or two don't worry and you can text or video call me all you want until then." I reassure her by turning in my seat to look back at her and rub on her cheek. I can feel Haze staring a hole in the side of head since we haven't talked much since our first night and I still haven't read the letter.

"Don't worry princess we will be pulling up on Goddy and your sister and brother in a week I already have the time off." He informs her but more so me as he looks at her in the rear view mirror. All I can do is shake my head at his antics. We all hop out the truck and of course I have to wait until he comes around to open my door.

"Sapphire, you have until then to read that letter and wrap your head around what's in it then I'm yo ass like a gnat on a horses ass. Fight me if you want, I have things to tame bratty women baby." He whispers directly into my ear in his husky voice causing tingles to run down my spine and goosebumps raise on my arms as I close my eyes and take in his scent one last time. I may read this letter, but I don't see things changing between us, my family would have a damn fit if they found out I was dating Haze no matter how long it's been since Monique died. Growing up so close with the golden grandchild had some perks but it was more of a catch twenty-one with me being the black sheep's daughter and my aunt Farah, Monique's mom, being the golden child as well. They could do no wrong in my grandparent's eyes and my mom was not for the bullshit.

"Get out of your head Sapphire. I said what I meant and fuck yo family if they have a problem with it. Now give me a hug and our babygirl with her pouty face." He chuckles but I still hear the sternness in his voice as he wraps his large smooth dark chocolate tattooed arms around me. I can't help but lean into his embrace laying my head on his chest as I wrap my arms around his waist, and we stand there for a minute. I swear I can feel his emotions roll off him in waves causing my body to heat up. He finally releases me, and I give Harmony a much needed hug and kiss, still promising to see her soon. Our flight back home was quick as I always booked straight shot tickets in first class, I could careless about the price tag I already hated to fly.

Chapter Four

Hazekiel "Haze" Jenkins

It's been a few days since Sapphire and the kids left and our home has felt empty since. I can even see the sadness in my babygirl even though she has been on the phone with them every moment she can. I've been texting and calling Phire but keeping it light talk so she doesn't feel pressured even if part of me wants to hop on the next flight, wait for her in her room with the letter open on the bed, a box of tissue, and maybe sedative and cuffs cause I'm sure she is going to lose her shit heavy when she reads what that evil bitch wrote. I am still wondering how were we even friends back then but the saying a wolf in sheep's clothing rings true. I received some good news this morning before starting the cadet training, I finally got the approval for my early retirement, so next month is my last I must go in. I haven't told either of my loves just yet I'm planning that surprise for when we are on our family trip for Harmony's birthday. It was never in my plans to be a career military officer, I was just following my dad's lead with learning what I can and it did provide a legal way to provide for the family that was dropped in my lap during my gap year before I shipped out.

2008

"Haze, I have a serious problem and only you can fix it."
Monique bust into my bedroom like her dramatic ass usually does but today she seemed like she was actually in distress with her clothes disheveled and hair sticking to her sweaty

forehead, so I turn from my computer to give her my full attention.

"Breath girl what the hell is wrong?" I question as she closes my door then flops down on my queen sized bed.

"I'm pregnant." She rushes out fidgeting with her fingers looking around like someone could hear what she just confessed to me but with both my doctor parents still being at the hospital and my brother away at college we were all alone.

"What the fuck Monique your parents are going to kill you." My voice boomed as I jumped from my seat after registering everything she actually said.

"I know that's why I need your help and you're going to give it friend."

"How the hell can I help you with this? What you want me to take you to get an abortion or something?" I looked at her puzzled and hopeful that was all she wanted me to do.

"NO why would I get rid of my baby? I want you to tell my parents that it's yours and we're getting married. They love you and have always hinted at wanting us to be together so why not make it official, please best friend?" I stared at her a few moments tilting my head and squinting like she had grown another damn head or at least bumped hers because there was no way in hell I was agreeing to this shit show especially not after finally getting Sapphire to agree with me enlisting and finally letting our relationship be known.

"You out yo damn mind Mo. Why in the hell would I agree to any of that, and you know how I feel about Sapphire, and I

won't betray her like that. Now I can help you figure something else out, like where is the father?"

"Sapphire... Sapphire... Sapphire. I'm your best friend how the hell did you fall for my cousin, any damn way? You know what don't answer that shit it doesn't matter you will do it you don't have a choice because if you don't, I'll gladly tell your lil secret." She looks at me with the evilest dark eyes I've ever seen, and I can't believe this is the friend I was making mud pies with in elementary school.

PRESENT

"Daddy... Daddy..." Harmony shouts from the backseat snapping me out of my thoughts.

"Yes baby?" I ask clearing my throat.

"We're here we're at gma and pawpaw's house." She bounces in her seat ready to hop out, but she knows to always wait for me to open her door for her. I turn my head and realize that sure enough I have driven on autopilot to my parents townhouse they moved in once I took over the family home. I hopped out my truck and went to open her door, which the moment it is fully open she jumps out giving me a quick peck on the cheek and dashes off to jump in my dad's arms. For a sixty five year old man he could go for my brother instead with his six foot four inches two hundred slim fit frame and salt and pepper hip length locs. We still work out together twice a week and he runs every morning with my mom by his side. My parents have been together happily for over forty years, and I always wanted that for myself and just knew Sapphire was the one I would be living out that dream with.

"Hey son why you look so out of it?" My dad questions as I walk to their front porch still zoning out.

"Just a lot on my mind pops." I didn't feel like getting into my true feelings right now when I know in a few days all hell is going to break loose soon anyways.

"Would it happen to be due to a certain rare stone named young lady that left last weekend?" He inquires as we sit down in his office and the women go to the family room.

"No why would it be about Sapphire?"

"Maybe because you have been single for a while and in love with her since middle. Hell, I never understood why you married Monique anyways. I mean she was your best friend and all, but something was never quite right with that child." I look at my dad dumbfounded because I never expressed my feelings for her to anyone after that day.

"How did you know I had feelings for her and wait what do you mean you don't know why I married Monique?" The only people that knew Harmony wasn't mine were our friend group of six and none of them were around much after high school.

"Haze you are my son of course I know who you really loved, and I love Harmony so does your mother, but we knew years ago she wasn't actually your daughter. We were waiting for you to finally stop pretending." He explains sipping on some cognac he poured himself and handed me my glass. I'm close with both of my parents and rarely hide anything from them. I idolized them both so much growing up because even with their busy careers they always made time for my brother and I as well as each other.

34

"I don't even know what to say pops, but things were complicated back then hell they still are and probably about to get crazy for a bit. I just-"

"No need to explain son whatever happens me and your mother always have your back, but I hope apart of the craziness is you going after the woman you love finally. You shouldn't be alone because you did something out of loyalty or stupidity years ago." He reassures me by placing his hand on my shoulder and squeezing as he spoke. We talked for a bit more and in all honesty, I should have come to my dad about this long ago he always helps get my thoughts straight. Harmony is staying at my parents for a couple days since this weekend we will be at Sapphire's, and they haven't had their weekend with her which is something they are adamant about. Pulling in to the garage my phone rings with a video call from Sapphire and if she's calling by video either she has finally decided to read the letter and is about to go off or she's about to and just wants me on the phone.

"Hi baby what's going on?" I answer.

"Hi Haze, I see you aren't giving up so I might as well read the letter since it's been burning a hole in my suitcase the past few days." She sighs and it looks like she hasn't been sleeping much.

"Baby I hate seeing you so stressed. You look like you haven't slept much. We can do this another day just go draw you a bath, light you some candles, and relax."

"It's not your fault. I've felt something was off for years but just ignored it. It's time to get answers." She props her phone on a pillow in front of her as she sits cross-legged in front of it. I watch as she slowly opens up the letter and starts to read it out loud.

THE LETTER

Dear Cuz,

If you're reading this, cancer finally took me out—but not before I said my peace. I know you'll hate me after this, and I honestly don't care. I was jealous from the day you moved here, parading around with your long hair, nerdy glasses, and that big ass like you owned the place. Haze was mine, but you just *had* to take him. Whatever—I got him in the end. Call it what you want, but he was mine, even if he never loved me. I forced that marriage, yeah. How? Easy. I knew his secret. I followed him one night to where he murdered Varius by the lake, slit his throat over *you*. I watched him dump the body like trash. So, when I got pregnant, I didn't know whose it was, I made my move. I told him to marry me, or I'd go to the cops. I didn't have any proof, but I knew just enough to scare him. I thought he'd fall for me someday. Instead, he treated me like air, obsessed with you while I faded. You ruined everything, but guess what? I still won. That's all I have for you well besides mommy dearest is holding something back. That's all. Bye, bitch.

"You gotta be fuckin kidding me. I loved this stupid bitch. I helped take care of her ass the whole time she was sick, but she hates me for someone who never fuckin wanted her!!" She screams with tears sliding down her beautiful chocolate cheeks and it's breaking my heart that I can't comfort her right now. I pull up flights on my computer while simultaneously reaching out to my commander and fellow trainer about covering my training for the next two days since I wasn't scheduled for the weekend any. She's up pacing the floor mumbling to herself. I let her pace as I start packing a bag and messaging my parents that I need to leave and since I told them about the letter and they already knew about my feelings for Sapphire it wasn't hard for them to get why I needed to leave.

"Baby come to the camera please." I plead with her as I hop on my motorcycle to head to the airport to take the redeye, I was able to book.

"What Haze?" She is crying so hard her normal bright hazel eyes are red and puffy.

"I'm on my way to you now my parents will fly in with Harmony this weekend. I know it's a lot, but we will get through it together." I reassure her as I speed through traffic to cut the normal thirty to forty minute drive to the airport down to twenty even if my flight doesn't leave for another hour and a half.

"I don't think that's such a good idea. I need time to process this shit. Like my own damn cousin extorted you to be with her just so you wouldn't be with me because she was obsessed with you. Then you... you-"

"I know it's a lot Sapphire that's why I'm on the next flight to you so I can help you process all this mess and answer any questions you may have. I'm pulling up to extended parking now. I scheduled a car pickup, so you don't have to worry about coming to get me. I'll call you when I'm close."

"Ok Haze, I will see you when you get here. I just used my sick days for tomorrow well today and Friday anyways there is no way I can think straight right now."

"Good grab you a bottle of wine and relax. I should be there in about six hours. I love you, Sapphire." I knew she wouldn't say it back, not yet but I had to let her know how I'm feeling. We end the call as I reach security check in line which being that it's after midnight not that many people are coming in for flights.

Chapter Five

Sapphire Bentley

I have been pacing the floor and cursing since I got off the phone with Haze. Clearly the wine didn't help as I'm on my second bottle and I have read that damn letter three more times hoping what I read the first time was all in my head, but it wasn't. I decide to make us some breakfast since he just text me to say he just landed. I let him know the door is unlocked since I'm making pancakes and I'm not trying to burn them. I seriously need something to soak up all this wine I've drank. Soon I hear a knock at the door and stupidly scream it's open instead of checking the camera first and it didn't register that I told him it would be unlocked so he wouldn't knock. When I turn to the person entering into my damn kitchen, I wish I would have checked first cause the kids father is the last damn person I want to see right now.

"Malakhi what the hell are you doing here and at six in the damn morning?" I question my sorry ass baby daddy who the kids haven't seen in over three years since he found his little fiancé.

"Don't be like that Sapphire. I came to see the kids and you of course. Are they up yet?" He asks looking around as he takes a seat at my island. I used to love me some Malakhi. I was the nerd in college, and he was the student athlete, but he was getting a degree in law. I really thought we were going to be great together until he decided to sign his contract our junior year instead of finishing his degree. Feeling like a single mother while we were still together, constant traveling, and women throwing themselves at him with him indulging in them amongst other things I decided to leave.

"Well, if you would have called before just showing up then you would know the kids aren't even here, they are with my parents. So, you can leave now."

"Can we talk for a bit?" I can see in his grey eyes he is up to something and whatever he wants to talk about will just piss me off even more than I already am with this Monique shit. Oh shit, Haze and as soon as that thought enters my mind, I hear the door chime from someone opening the front door. When Malakhi turns and his eyes meet with Haze, I feel the tension in the room jump to a good twenty. The two of them are similar in build with Haze being a few inches taller than Malakhi and Haze being on the darker side plus so much more muscular too. Haze has this blank look on his face making it hard to read if he is mad or not, but he calmly puts his bag down by the steps and continues his walk to me never taking his eyes off Malakhi.

"Hi baby I didn't know we were going to have company." He finally greets me, leaning down to kiss the top of my head as he pulls me into his side with his arm around my waist. I can't do anything but smile because it feels so good being in his arms plus the look on Malakhi's face is priceless, which also further confirms he is here on some bullshit.

"Wait Sapphire isn't this ya cousins husband well widow? Why the fuck is he calling you baby and putting his hands all on you?" He shouts, jumping from his seat at the island. I really hoped he wouldn't remember him after only seeing him a few times at family functions over the years we were together and when he decided to pop up to play dad.

"Don't worry about all that. You have yet to say why you're even popping up at my damn house." I counter trying to change the subject and move out of Haze's arms, but he isn't having it.

"I was here to talk about us being a family again but clearly you to busy being a hoe chasing ya own dead cousins leftovers around." Before I can even react, Haze is around the island with his hand around Malakhi's throat lifting him in the air. It takes me a moment to even register his movements because I'm too busy gawking at his massive tattooed arms and the veins bulging from his huge hands that are wrapped around his neck. His damn white t-shirt looks as if it is painted on his glowing dark chocolate skin.

"Haze please put him down." I finally snap out of my trance when I hear Malakhi gasping for air and trying to get out of Haze's grip. I lightly touch Haze's shoulder, and he finally looks down at me then simply drops him like he weighs nothing at all.

"You need to leave Malakhi and even if he wasn't here the answer to your asinine thought of us being a family again would be no. If you wanted to be a family, you'd come get ya kids more often or at least call."

"You heard her nigga leave, don't make her repeat herself." Haze demands pulling me behind him as he looks down at Malakhi still rubbing his neck sitting on the floor. He finally gets the picture getting up to leave but still having a stare down with Haze.

"You ok baby?" He turns to me placing his hand under my chin lifting my head to meet his eyes when we hear the door latch and chime that it's been closed. This time I remember to check the camera and see him get into his car clearly pissed off.

"I'm ok. I made us breakfast." I inform him trying to turn around but he wraps me in his arms, squeezing me tight, and kissing the top of my head. We stand there for a minute or two with my head on his chest just inhaling his woodsy vanilla scent mixed with his natural scent slowly making my pussy wet. This is one day I wish I put on underwear walking around my house in my moomoo.

"I could hold you in my arms forever and it still wouldn't be long enough Phire. Come on let's eat it's smelling good in here." He expresses tapping me on my ass and kissing the top of my head again. I make our plates, and we eat in silence for a few minutes.

"So, you're the reason we never saw Varius again after that summer." I finally speak asking the first thing that comes to mind.

"He should have never put his hands on you. Is me killing him a problem for you?" He puts his fork down looking me right in the eyes as if trying to read my mind.

"No, not at all Varius was a piece of shit. I just wish you would've checked your surroundings better when dealing with his ass." I continue to eat calmly because I truly did not care that he killed his sorry ass. It actually turns me on a bit to know he would really kill for me. I mean you hear men say they would about their women or family, but he truly did it without a second thought. Maybe that makes me just as crazy as he must be but I'm cool with that.

"Wait really? Well I don't want us to have any secrets so would you be mad if I said it's about two of your exes and that stupid ass nigga that stayed next to y'all in your old building that didn't understand the word no down there with him?" Now that shocked my ass and not because he did it but I'm just now realizing I never told this fool where I lived before or now.

"Haze how did you know my address and that I even lived in a building before this?" I grilled him and he never broke eye contact.

"I've always known where you are whether I had someone check on you or I found you myself. I told you woman I've always been in love with you, and it was always in my plans to come get you whether your cousin Mo's ass died or not. Finding that letter a year ago just helped me put my plan in motion and gave me more hope you wouldn't turn me away."

"I still don't know about us. My life has been peaceful since moving here and this will cause a shit storm but a part of me wants to try just to spite that conniving parasite of a cousin, but I don't want to start a relationship that way."

"It's ok baby we can take things slow. I've waited over ten years to even be this close I can wait a bit longer." He walks around the island to stand in front of me as I turn to look up at him.

"Two conditions first."

"Name it."

43

"No more killing people and we don't say anything to the kids unless things become serious."

"Agreed when it comes to the kids but the killing people baby if anyone threatens our family, they are ending up in my grandparents lake with the rest of em."

"Maybe change that spot then, I don't need you getting caught." He just nods his head then leans down ghosting his lips across mines at first then sealing them together with a kiss that has my juices sliding down my inner thigh and my body heating up like a volcano getting ready to blow. I place a hand on either side of his face as he grabs me by the waist lifting me up onto the island causing my dress to hike up then centering himself between my legs not breaking the kiss for a second.

"Mhmm Haze we're supposed to be taking things slow remember." I remind him when he releases me long enough to take a breath.

"I fully intend to after I dig in them guts in a minute. You should have never wore this silky shit showing off that fat ass with no drawers on. Feel how hard you make me baby." He moans into my ear taking one of my hands and placing it on his very and I mean very large dick through his sweatpants. He starts kissing and sucking on my neck and I can't hold the moan that leaves my lips. His dick feels so good in my hands, but I am wondering how in the hell is all of it going to fit in me.

"Tell me now if you really don't wants this because once I enter this pussy, you're mines but we can take it as slow as you need." He makes me look him in the eyes as his hand travels up my dress and glides over my swollen bud and my juices cover his fingers. I scoot to the edge of the island using the hand that was on his third leg to pull down his pants enough to free it then line it up with entrance. When I rub it across, I instantly feel the piercing in the head of his dick, and he gets a mischievous smirk on his face.

"You know what that is?" I just nod because I am completely speechless and so turned on, I think I just came on myself.

"Words my little Phire." He commands grabbing me by the neck and pulling me closer.

"Yes... Yes, I want this, and you have a Prince Albert piercing." I say just above a whisper trying to scoot further so he would enter me but he's holding firm with one on my hip.

"That's my girl. Hmmm fuck you are so wet for me baby." He places one of my legs in each of his arms then starts to enter me slowly and the stretch that is happening takes my breath completely away.

"Phire breathe. There you go. Damn this pussy so tight baby, relax for me."

"Haze it's so big, I don't think it's going to fit ba... babe it's been so long." I moan trying to relax my muscles because this man's dick is so damn big, and I've had some big dicks in my life. He becomes fully seated in my pussy and this man head is hitting my cervix with his Prince Albert piercing rubbing on my G-spot.

"Fuck baby I knew this shit would feel good but damn. Sapphire you can never leave. Even after I'm gone, I will plague your every dream until the day we reunite in the afterlife, do you understand me?" He expresses with his hand around my neck staring me in my eyes making my pussy gush around his
45

long hard dick. I know some women may say run this man is crazy but he's crazy about me and that's fine with me. Let me be honest though after finally getting him I wouldn't hesitate to make a few bitches pick and dig their own graves before I put them in it. He starts giving me these long slow strokes, and my eyes roll in the back of my head.

"Fu... fucckkkk." I stutter coming for the third time this morning. He slides out of me then smacks his thick dick against my swollen sensitive bud. Haze pushes me back on the counter with his hand in the middle of my chest then drops down on one knee sucking my already sensitive clit in between his lips doing circles around it with the tip of his tongue. I buck against his mouth needing more and he gives me just that letting go my clit to flatten his tongue over it rubbing up and down then licking from my clit down to my entrance then licking around it. He inserts his tongue swirling it around and creating a suction like he's trying to draw out my soul from my damn pussy.

"Sh...shi...shiiittt Haze don't stop. I'm cumming." I scream as my legs start to tremble, my breathing gets heavy, and my body starts to tingle from my toes to me head making me feel lightheaded. He goes back to my clit nibbling on it then sucking to ease the pain. I do something I've never done before, I squirt, and he swallows every bit licking a few times then standing pushing his dick deep inside me in one swift move pushing until he's hitting my cervix again.

"Damn babe you even taste amazing. That next nut I need you to hold it till I say so."

"Ze you feel to good I don't know if I can." I moan and yelp as he lifts me from the counter like I way nothing at all.

"You're going to hold it cause you're my good girl." He starts lifting me and dropping me hard on his dick repeatedly then holding me with just the tip still in.

"You're doing sooo good baby. This pussy is so warm and gushy. You hear that?" Haze brings me up and down but not fulling entering me and I hear the sticky sounds of my cum.

"Sir I need to come please...pleasssseee." I plead with him as I feel my orgasm right on the edge.

"Come for me Sapphire but keep your eyes on me." My orgasm hits me so hard it feels like I'm floating as I fight to keep my eyes on him. It continues to wash over me as I feel him cum, and tears start to slide down my cheeks. I feel his legs twitch like they are about to give out.

"Don't worry I got you baby. That was amazing though." He expresses breathlessly.

"It truly was and now I need a nap." I giggle and we head upstairs to shower then do just that.

Chapter Six

Hazekiel "Haze" Jenkins

Waking up with her finally in my arms has me feeling like my world axis has been set right. I was fully prepared for her to put up a fight in us being together but clearly, I underestimated just how much she truly wanted me and the effect that letter would have on her. I'm laying here watching her sleep, rubbing circles on her exposed arm while we spoon hoping she still feels the same when she wakes.

"Mhmm." She moans coming awake then rubbing her body against mines.

"Sorry baby I didn't mean to wake you, your skin just feels sooo good under my fingertips."

"It's ok. I'm just glad you're really here and that wasn't just a dream." I wrap my arm around her tighter just pleased she's still happy about us.

"So that means no regrets?"

"No regrets Haze. I do have some questions though."

"Anything Sapphire."

"What took you so long to come for me?" I move to sit up with my back on the headboard and I pull her with me then she places her head on my chest.

"I wanted things to be as perfect as possible when I finally came, and I wanted to give you time to grieve your loss. Even after she died, I was still being deployed just not as much. I've only been a trainer the past four years and if you remember I only found the letter about a year ago. When I found out and read it, I wasn't in a good head space afterwards. I was already living the reality that someone I called my best friend since childhood blackmailed me into marrying them but then to find out that yea she knew but all the proof was a lie to keep me away from you but it made sense why I never found any and believe me I looked. I just couldn't imagine what else she might be capable of, so I never took the chance." I explain the best I can without letting the pure rage take over again.

"Wait we didn't use a condom babe." She jumps up in a panic and I grab her to lay back down.

"You don't have to worry about anything I haven't had sex in over two years, and I had a vasectomy right after we signed the marriage license at the courthouse. I was not going to risk actually impregnating her."

"I know it may be crazy to ask but did you guys have sex?"

"It's not baby and yes, a few times her and there after one of her mandatory date night's. She showed me this photo, that I now know was bogus, once at the beginning threatening to send it to the police if I didn't agree to take her out at least twice a month when I was stateside." I feel myself getting pissed again and I start clenching my fist. Sapphire notices the shift in my energy and gives me a kiss on my chest then wraps her arms around me as much as she can. That simple gesture just calmed me quicker than any technique my therapist has taught me and yes, I have a damn therapist if I didn't a lot more people would be dead.

"I still can't wrap my head around the fact she really blackmailed you into marrying her and to have sex with her, but she claims she loved you, that's some straight bullshit. You don't hurt people you love like that." She shakes her head on my chest as I'm rubbing circles on her back.

"I almost understand that but her hate for you is what I don't get. You were always good to her even when she was on some passive aggressive shit with you."

"Thinking back on it now I am remembering lil snide comments she would make or off hand looks especially if you were near me before and after that whole debacle of a marriage. One last thing though is there anything else you may need to tell me?"

"Ummm well there is the slight situation of you buying this house from me well from my company and I'm the one that upgraded the security system before you moved in."

"HAZEEE!!" She pops up off my chest and hits me shaking her head.

"Look you were living in those not so safe apartments with the kids and I already had to eliminate one dumb ass neighbor for fuckin with you so when I got word you were looking for homes, I made this one available. It was the best fit for you and the kids along with me and Harmony once I came for my family."

"So, you've really been stalking me all these years?"

"I call it keepin you safe but yes, I have and will always. But on the family tip what's up with this nigga Malakhi, is he going to be a problem?" I look at her with raised eyebrows. I know that nigga hasn't been around for a few years now, so something must be up if he's popping up again and I'm going to find out what real fast.

"Honestly this time I don't know what made him show up on that tip. I haven't seen or spoken to him other than on the kids birthday last year when he called to say happy birthday and break another promise to them. The last I knew though he was getting married." We lay there for a while longer just talking about any and everything until our stomachs start to growl. We end up ordering in after seeing the kitchen mess we had to clean up. Back comfortably in the bed watching a movie her phone starts to ring with a call from her mom.

"Hey ma everything ok?"

"Yea baby I was just making sure I told you about the get together at your grandparents back home next weekend. The kids just told me y'all just came from there last week visiting Harmony and Haze though." I can hear the tone in her voice this conversation might be going left.

"Ok cool I have plenty of airline points to use and off on the weekend so if you really want to go, I will go for you but yea we had a long overdue fun visit with them. I really missed my girl." She mouths and you to me while moving the phone from her ear to smooch her lips for a kiss and I happily oblige.

"Is she the only one you missed and girl they are your grandparents don't act like that." Yup there it goes. We could never get anything pass Mrs. Bentley when we were growing up and clearly not now.

"Ma don't start and when it comes to those so call grandparents you know I'm good on that along with majority of that family."

"Oh, baby girl I'm not going to get into all that because I don't want to upset you more than what I'm about to say next. So that sorry ass Malakhi called me shouting about Haze walking up in your house like he owns the place kissing all on you then putting his hands on him, what's that all about?" She questions and I had a feeling it was coming.

"Ma you know I refrain from lying to you but yes Haze is here because there are somethings we recently found out and he came to be here for me and the rest we are still figuring out. I'm not ready to get into details yet."

"Oooh baby you finally got your man. I never understood why he married Mo's evil ass, and she wonders why she was adopted." She mumbles that last part, and we can barely make it out. It was no secret that she was adopted after Sapphire's aunt and uncle were having fertility issues.

"Wait mama you're not disappointed or mad at me? I know this is going to cause some drama, but I love him, always have." She shrugs her shoulders with a small grin.

"Don't you think I know that. It's the reason me and your aunt got into it all those years back. It was the same day she told me about them going to the courthouse to get married and about Harmony. I knew something wasn't right but when you are ready to tell us we'll be waiting with open arms and hearts. You were always my son Haze and always will be." That declaration made my heart smile and clearly made my woman emotional by the tears sliding down her mocha high cheekbones. I kissed each one and she smiles.

"Thank you, mama. You just don't know how much that means to me, but it's been a long day. I need some sleep and to prepare for Haze's parents coming over with Harmony tomorrow."

"Really, they all are coming over. Don't worry, they can all stay here with your dad and me. You know him and Mr. Jenkins use to be as thick as thieves back in the day but gone head and enjoy y'all alone time we have the kids, later my babies."

"Later ma." We said in unison then laughing at our own antics. We lay there in a comfortable silence with the occasional laugh at whatever was on the tv.

"Hazekiel." Shit she called my government name; some shit I haven't heard this much since my early military days.

"Yes baby?"

"You're coming with me to this stupid get together. I know what we said-"

"Say less baby." I declared cutting her off and kissing the top of her head as it rests on my chest. She smooches her lips for a kiss that I will never get tired of giving.

Chapter Seven

Sapphire Bentley

Before I knew it next weekend was here, and we were all loading into Haze's Tahoe my parents included. We were heading straight to his parents as that is where my parents decided to stay since we all know the shit is about to hit the fan when we all pull up to my grandparents tomorrow afternoon.

"Aww there go all my grandbabies." Mrs. Jenkins exclaims like she didn't just see them all last weekend. I am still shocked and appreciative about how loving and accepting they are of my kids, but I shouldn't be surprised after Haze explained that his parent's always knew that Harmony wasn't biologically his. They all embraced each other with warm loving hugs and at that moment I kinda envied my kids because I wished I had that love from my only living grandparents. My dad's parents died before I was born in this big accident that happened on the turnpike, he always says God meant for it to happen that way because they wouldn't be able to live happily without each other, that's just how in love they were. Mrs. Jenkins wraps me up in a hug next leaning down to kiss me on the cheek, I swear his whole family is tall as hell.

"Uhhh Gemini our two babies have finally gotten out of their own ways and set our families like they always should have been." Mr. Jenkins says to my dad giving me a tight hug and making me giggle when I hear Haze clearing his throat next to me then grabbing my hand then pulling me into his side. They both burst into a bolsters of laughter with their Barry White deep voices.

"Yup that's your boy and I couldn't ask for a better man to protect my princesses and prince." My dad chuckles coming around to squeeze Haze's shoulder then clapping hands with Mr. Jenkins and then pulling him into a one-armed bro hug. By this time the kids are already outside playing in the playground that can be seen from their back porch. What this community lacked in yard space for each townhome, it made up for it with amenities. I go to grab my parents bags but I am quickly stopped by Haze and our fathers.

"Y'all go relax we will take those upstairs after we finish watching the kids play themselves to hunger then sleep baby." I just nod and smile after he pulls me in for a quick kiss then heading out back with our smiling dads.

"Now that's love babygirl." My mom declares all smiles as we take a seat at the large island and Mrs. Jenkins goes to stirring up whatever she is cooking then hands each of us a wine glass.

"I haven't seen my baby boy so happy in years, but I know with your family Trinity shit won't be easy for them." She says leaning forward on the island with her glass between her hands.

"Yea I'm hoping it won't be too bad tomorrow but who knows. Sometimes I wonder why I even deal with most of them these days but I'm sure it's because I don't live here anymore and only come back occasionally." I nod my head in agreement because my mother literally spends her days with my dad, at her wine or book club, or me and the kids. We have family night at least eight times a month when her and my dad aren't traveling or off separate with one of the kids. We chat for a bit longer but soon in come the kids complaining about being

55

hungry and we send them off to clean up while we fix the plates. Haze comes up behind me with his massive hand covering my side and kisses me on the cheek after making sure the kids actually used soap to wash their hands.

"You ok baby?"

"Yea I'm just tired." I answer leaning my head back on his chest after handing the now seated kids their plates and they dig in the moment amen leaves their mouths.

"We can take our food to go. You do look exhausted baby." He kisses the top of my head and starts moving around the kitchen to pack our food as I kiss my babies who are not paying me much attention anyways. After letting our moms know we're leaving I hear our dads coming down the stairs.

"Aw princess you two leaving already?" My dad questions when he notices the to-go bag in Haze's hands.

"Yes, dad I need some sleep." He just nods ok and pulls me in for one of his infamous daddy bear hugs I love so much. Mr. Jenkins does the same before they both switch giving their see you laters to Haze. Once we make it back to his home I head straight for the shower, and he soon joins me.

"I'll never get enough of having you in my arms like this." He expresses as he wraps his large arms around me resting my back on his front after turning another shower head on to get his back. The shower starts to steam up but it's not like suffocating heat, it's so relaxing.

"You know I'm not too tired." I drive my point home by reaching behind me to stroke his already hard as a brick third leg, rubbing my thumb over his Prince Albert piercing that's resting on my ass. He leans down to my ear moaning and bites my neck then licks the same spot sending chills down my spine right to my honey pot that is so ready for him to fill me up.

"I have something better. Just remember you're the one that said you weren't tired." He takes the washcloth I grabbed before getting in, then proceeds to wet it and suds it up with this sweet but citrus smell that he ordered for me. He actually bathes me from the neck down paying extra attention to my pussy.

"Now that your clean sit there until I finish washing up." He commands and I have a seat on the shower seat as he directs. I lean back to watch his back muscles flex with every movement and the white suds glide down his dark mocha skin. My clit starts to throb as I continue to take in every scar adorning his body. When I make it down to his tight plump ass, I damn near get up from my seat to grab it but decide to compose myself because I want to see what he has planned. I've been so conflicted with the time we lost, then just being grateful I have him and both our parents as well as the kids being happy, we're together. He turns around to rinse his back giving me a full view of his six pack, big chest, thick thighs, and lawwwdddd that dick. I'm still trying to comprehend how it even fit but considering I had two big head ass children come out of it, I guess I shouldn't be too surprised.

"I didn't notice this before, what happened? If you don't mind telling me of course." I jump up rushing to him to lightly glide my fingers over a particularly nasty looking scar on his left side and I notice the moment he stiffens. I drop my hand and look up into his eyes to see what emotion just came across them, but he masks them with lust and love real fast.

"I will tell you soon but now, I want you to get dried off and lay in the middle of the bed for me." He directs me then leans down to give me a quick peck on the lips and smacks my bare ass cheeks. I giggle stepping out the shower, grabbing my towel, and seductively drying off making sure to bend over with my ass facing him giving him full view of my glistening pussy. I crawl in the middle of his massive double king size bed and notice the blanket on the bed is not a regular comforter.

"It's called an intimacy blanket keeps that waterpark of a pussy from wetting up the bed." He grins walking into the closet to grab a red velvet box.

"You trust me?" He questions laying the box at my feet on the bed and I feel like I just set myself up for some seriously freaky shit. My nipples harden even further as the thought of what could be in that box and what he will do with them race through my mind like a track star.

"Do you."

"Oh yea... yes Haze, I trust you." I moan as he circles my right nipple with the tip of his finger.

"Your safe word Is Mercy." He informs me to saunter from my side to finally open that darn box that is plaguing my mind to find out what's in it. When he gets it unlocked with a key, I didn't even notice him pulling from his pocket. He turns the box towards me, and I go deer in headlights because this man has one engraved my name in the inner lid in gold and two the toys I have never tried before decorating the inside of the large box. He takes out the furry handcuffs, oil, and a sapphire blue silk blindfold. He closes the box placing it in an armchair by the window then comes back to my side placing the blindfold on me first kissing my lips as he ties it behind my head. Next I feel the handcuffs clamp around my wrist and something hooking between them and I can't help but tug at them.

"Ouch."

"Don't pull you will get pinched Phire. You are connected to the bed, so are you ready?"

"Yes Sir."

"Good girl." I feel his weight on the bed in between my legs then I hear the top come off the bottle of oil he has and all of a sudden vanilla and hints of cinnamon with something sweet hits my nose making me feel all tingly. He begins dropping oil on my body starting on my legs making a trail up them to just over my pussy, my stomach, around my thirty- eight H size breast, each arm, and ending at my neck where he leans in placing his juicy lips a top of mine for a sensual slow kiss spreading my lips with his tongue.

"Mhmm." I moan into his mouth wiggling my hips to get some type of friction attempting to ease the ache between my legs for him.

"Did I tell you to move yet?" He pops me on my thigh stopping our heated kiss. When he leans away my body feels warm all over and that's when I notice the oil must be self-heating. Not being able to see but feel everything is driving my damn senses crazy and I am hornier than I have ever been in my fuckin life. I feel him massaging my feet hitting that soft spot in the middle with just the right pressure. I can't help but let out another low moan. Haze massages my toes, my heels and my ankles making sure not to miss one tight spot before he moves up taking his time to massage each leg. When he finally finishes after peppering kisses everywhere he touches, he moves back to massaging my pussy and at this point I'm so relaxed yet aroused the first flick of my clit and I squirt all over his hand.

"Shit Haze. Please I need to feel you." I moan softly.

"Mhmm that was sexy as fuck. You will feel me soon enough my Phire but first I'm hungry." He groans, massaging my lips spreading them with his thumb. He circles my entrance dipping it in then taking it out. I hear him moan again.

"Fuck you taste like heaven baby. Don't you dare hold back. I don't care if I drown in your juices, it will be with a smile." Next thing I feel is his warm tongue sliding between my lips from my opening to clit flattening out then using the tip to circle my swollen bud and sucking it in between his soft lips. His damn suction with the quick flicks of tongue over my bud initiate my orgasm to crash into me like a head on car collision and I swear I see stars.

"HAAAZZZZEEE." I scream as he continues his assault on my pussy and my orgasm continues to roll over. I see why he put this damn blanket down because before I can think to hold it, I'm squirting all over his face and mouth as he latches back on to my clit swallowing every drop.

"Fu...fuucckkk." He has the damn nerve to moan as he's eating my pussy then adding two of his large fingers with his thumb rubbing my cum over my ass hole before he pushes it inside.

He finds a rhythm and I don't know how with the way I'm tossing my head from side-to-side moaning and bucking off the bed just plain delirious at this point. I know I am going to have bruising on my wrist by the time we are done because I damn sure as hell didn't listen and have been tugging at these damn things the way this man is sucking my soul from my clit. He finally let's go when my shaking subsides.

"That was one tasty fucking meal. It will definitely be on a daily meal rotation." He says but I can tell it's not a suggestion when he leans down kissing me with his lips that are coated in my juices. Sticking his tongue in my mouth I start to suck on it tasting myself and enjoying every bit.

"Now I've been wanting that fat ass in the air for a minute so it's time to roll over my thickness." He grabs me by my waist flipping me over as if I weigh nothing to him. I beat him to getting me on my knees then put a deep arch in my back shaking my ass in his face.

"I want to see you twerk that fat ass on this dick, so no running Phire." He says smacking me on both my ass cheeks at the same time and damn that shit stung, but I like it. I feel the oil dripping over my back then my ass and finally the back of my legs. When the warm sensation starts, I can't help but wiggle my ass as the chills run down my spine and right to my pussy. He's a little bit quicker with this massage but still got every kink in my body especially my arms since they have been in this position for a while now. Just when I feel the last muscle in my body relax, he rubs his third leg between my pussy lips inciting a deep moan to leave me. We've had sex a few times now, but I still feel the stretch in my pussy walls every time.

"This tight shit right here will be the death of someone thinking they can touch what's mine. Damn woman." He groans as he pushes in so deep his piercing is tickling my cervix in this angle. Apart of me is so fuckin turned on by his declaration and the other is worried about making sure he covers his damn tracks properly. I know I shouldn't be condoning his behavior but it's so sexy actually having a man that will kill for me and about me.

"Oooh fuck rig... right there Haze."

"That's my woman take all this dick. Mmm shit just like that. You trying to make me cum already damn." Him egging me on makes me throw my ass back more, giving him the twerking on his dick he requested. I simultaneously clinch my walls around his length with every drop and lift of my ass. He leans forward finally taking the blind fold off my eyes and it takes a moment for them to adjust to the dim light in his room.

"When I cum I want those pretty eyes on me baby." He grunts slamming into my pussy over and over until my orgasm is knocking into me like the waves in a wave pool. It slows then he pushes deep inside me leaning forward to unhook me from the bed but leaving my hands cuffed pulling them behind me, he clearly remembers I'm double jointed, as he flips me on my side. Haze grabs one leg placing it on his shoulder with the other between his legs and pushes deep inside me again while biting into my calf. It feels like such a weird sensation at first then he does it again but leans forward and bites the back of my thigh and dammit I did not know that was a sensitive spot for me. Before I can even think about it, I am cumming all over his dick and it spills out onto our legs with each deep slow stroke he gives me. He does it a few more times, eliciting a back-to-back squirt session wetting both of us up.

"My freaky lil slut likes being bitten, noted. Ugghhh fuck I'm about to nut baby."

"Cum in yo pussy baby." I direct him moaning my own release when his starts to spill all over my walls.

"Fuck Phire." He grunts while he is still slow stroking until he goes soft, and he catches his breath. Finally, uncuffing me my arms fill so stiff, and I feel the scars on my wrist from the cuffs.

"Shit baby I'm so sorry I should've gotten some different cuffs your wrist are all red and bruised." He places kisses on each one.

"It's ok babe nothing a little cream and wrap won't heal. I have leather band bracelets I can where over them for tomorrow." He groans lightly rubbing them and kissing them again. It's only about nine o clock so we take another quick shower then head downstairs to warm up our food. While eating I can't help my mind from drifting to Monique's last few days.

2017

Shit last night was a rough one. I feel so sick to my stomach with myself that my first thought was about him and if he is safe across seas but all these years later, I still can't help it sometimes. At first I was hesitant about staying here to help my aunt take care of Monique but then I found out he was leaving on a mission which I was partially shocked about seeing as the doctors told us this week her last round of chemo did nothing, which I figured it wouldn't. The tumors growing on her lungs are getting larger and spreading but they want to revisit the surgical

63

route again. I get my hygiene together and head down the hall stopping to peak my head in on Monique who looks to be sleeping, so I keep heading to the kitchen.

"Good morning auntie." I greet Monique's mom and my mom sister Farah.

"Morning Sapphire. I already gave her... her meds. I have to run some errands I will be back later." She informs me placing the dish rag on the rack to dry, never even looking back at me. I swear I'll never understand why she is so cold to me compared to my other aunts. She walks out without another word, and I proceed to make me some breakfast since apparently, she only cooked for them. Moving my way through the kitchen I hear the alarm for the IV bag going off, so I turn everything off and head to her room. I've been doing this for so long I can tell the difference in the machines by the noise they make. Malakhi wasn't too happy about me leaving him with the kids since the season was over, but he would have to suck it up my family needed me. I love him though he has been the sweetest since we met my sophomore year of college. Well, I love him as much as I can. I'm pretty much on autopilot replacing her bag though and didn't even realize she was up.

"Hi Mo, how are you feeling? I figured you'd be out all morning."

"Ooofff that stupid alarm woke me up and the pain is getting worse. Where's my mother?" She coughs weakly and I hand her a cup of water trying to ease her throat irritation.

"She left to run some errands."

"Put some more of that morphine in this IV."

"Your mom already gave you some. You're not due for more for another four hours Mo." I turned my back to her rolling my eyes. I swear since she has been sick, she's even more fucking rude. I didn't mind the slick comments here and there when we were growing up which I'm sure they were only here and there because she knew I'd beat her ass if she tried me to hard. Now I think she thinks she will get a pass or something, but she keeps fucking with me. I love the bitch, but I take disrespect from nobody.

"You're fucking wit me right? I am dying! I'm in pain and you want to tell me about some damn meds sched-" She begins coughing violently and I watch for a minute then hand her some water. Once she calms down and turns over to go back to sleep, I leave the room to talk to my Malakhi. These past few days have been torture for the family as Mo has gotten worse as the doctors predict she may die if she didn't go ahead with the surgery soon.

PRESENT

"Come back to me baby." Haze leans down speaking into my ear as he's caressing my cheek so lovingly.

"I'm here." I lean into his touch loving the feel of his massive hands touching me so gently.

"Don't let her sink back in we have enough shit to deal with tomorrow and then it's up from there. Just us and the family we choose to keep around. You trust me, don't you?"

"With my life." I declare that as he peers into my eyes and reading me like a book.

"Then let's get ready for bed and leave the bullshit for tomorrow." We clean the kitchen up, check in on the kids, I hop on my dick making his toes curl, and then we finally get some rest. This morning I'm on autopilot and I feel Haze watching my every move. I trust him, I do it's not what he thinks and I'm clearly going to have to tell him what's really bothering me. We meet at his parents' home since we all wanted to arrive there together. It really feels good to have our parents on our side along with our babies. Driving down our families road is bittersweet. Growing up here was cool and encompassed with love. My grandparents home is the largest sitting on the right side of the street, then the four houses next to them are split between my aunts, as well as my grandmothers sister and her daughter, then across the street are my parents old home that my brother and his family lives in, Mo's parents are next to them, and it just goes on and on for like three blocks in either direction. Some think I'm crazy for leaving my families land, but I just couldn't stand being under the shadow of the perfect granddaughter any longer even with her ass being dead. I notice a few of my cousins sitting out on the front porch drinking just shooting the shit and I just know they are about to go and run their mouths the moment I step out.

"Hey what did I tell you." Haze gently grabs me by the chin to turn my head towards him after parking the truck.

"I'm ok Haze I promise. I just don't think it was a good idea to bring the kids with us since we know it's about to be some mess."

"Mom we're good and we have you and pops back." Dontrell speaks up from the back. You would think he's the oldest the way he always steps up for the girls and protects them.

"He's right Goddy. I'm glad you and my dad are together. I get you guys full time and he's happy, it's a win-win." Harmony speaks up next and Destiny just nods her head.

"See the kids are cool baby and listen when I say leave and go to the car kids I mean it." They all reply yes sir and we begin getting out of the truck. Of course, Haze walks over to open my door then holding my hand and giving me a quick peck on the lips before I fully hop out the truck.

"Hey the moment someone disrespects either of you we're out of here and don't ever have to come back, do you hear me?" My mom declares pining Haze and I in place with a look only a mother can give you and we just nod as we all walk off together with our parents walking behind us and the kids on either side. Haze refused to let my hand go or change his affection towards me in any way. We make it through the first hour with just four or five looks until Mo's parents show up and my grandparents come to sit in the back. The kids have just sat down, and we all decide to eat together at one of the picnic tables under the hut. I see the moment she notices us as Haze has his arm around my waist whispering something nasty in my ear and I giggle.

"Ut oh here comes my grandmother." Harmony whispers stuffing her mouth with food as she walks up on our table.

"Well, there's my babygirl, are you not going to come give me and your paw paw a hug?" Harmony doesn't say anything, but she gets up from sitting next to me and gives them a hug.

"Well, Hazekiel I would say it was nice to see you but what the hell is going on here?" She points between him and I. Both our parents walk up looking ready for war.

"Hey not in front of the kids let's go in the house." My mother suggests standing behind us with my dad next to her per usual.

"Yea let's." She responds. Haze lets the kids know to stay put and we walk into the house with my grandparents right behind us with a frown on their faces as Haze interlocks his fingers with mine. We head over to my grandfather's office on the other side of the house but with its tall double glass doors we can still see the backyard.

"So, you lil slut you just couldn't wait til my daughter was dead to go after her husband, could you?" She spits the moment the large office door shuts.

"Watch how you speak to her Mrs. Murphy." Haze immediately jumps to my defense even my mother grins impressed with his protective mode.

"Oh, really Hazekiel?" She whips her head around to look at him as she stands next to grandfather's desk as my grandmother stands on the opposite side right next to him. My uncle takes a seat in the corner of the office and our parents at their usual position.

"Look there clearly is a conversation that needs to be had but we will do it respectfully and with love as a family should now Sapphire what is going on here?" My grandfather laid down the law in his deep husky voice.

"Grandpa Haze and I were together before he and Mo ever got married. I recently read a letter written by her that explained

68

things about their marriage that I never understood to begin with, and we decided we wanted to be together like we should have been all along." I partially explain looking up at Haze.

"What do you mean explain their marriage? He knocked her up they were in love end of story." He asked.

"You've always been jealous of my baby and now you're standing here making up lies to make yourself feel better about sleeping with her husband."

"I never married Mo because I was in love with her nor is Harmony mines. She slept with two guys at a college party and didn't know which one was the father, so she decided to use a bit of information she knew about me to extort me into marrying her. The only person in this family I ever wanted and will marry is Sapphire. Mo was the one who was always jealous, Sapphire had nothing to be jealous of." They all gasp at the news and Haze's intentions of marriage except my uncle I notice. He has this look like he either knew all or at least part of what Haze just revealed to them.

"Lies Trenton do you not hear how they are talking about our baby." She turns to my uncle who's sitting in his seat to relaxed for my liking.

"I told you we should have never adopted her to begin with, but you wouldn't listen. You just had to have your daughter and the hell with who it hurt. I knew all about her promiscuous ways and knew about these two back then as well but oddly enough she is like you and had to one up her sister too."

"Wait what do you mean sister Uncle Trenton?" I asked stepping around Haze.

69

"Trenton that's not your business to tell so shut the hell up." My mother warns him.

"Somebody better tell me something. How would she be one upping her sister in this situation?" I demand starting to raise my voice hoping they aren't about to tell me what I think they are.

"Baby it's time she knows, clearly Monique figured it out at some point which make sense now." My dad informs my mom rubbing her shoulders.

"Fine Mo... Monique was your sister and my daughter." She says looking down at her feet and fidgeting with her fingers.

"How the hell? SO, YOU CHEATED ON MY DAD!?" I shout whipping my head back around looking between her and my dad.

"Baby calm down let her explain, come here." Haze tells me wrapping me in his arms with my back facing his chest and kissing my bare shoulder making me thankful I decided to wear my dark purple halter top so I can feel his soft lips, allowing them to calm me just a little bit.

"Yes, your mother is a slut just like you." My aunt blurts out causing my mom to slap the taste out of her mouth.

"I was raped you insufferable bitch and you know that. I'll never understand how you are our parents favorite." I gasp placing my hand over my mouth not really comprehending the fact that my mother just told me she was raped, and Mo is my sister.

"Don't start that mess, Trinity. She is not our favorite, she just listens more than you do but we love you both the same." My grandmother finally speaks up trying to defend their special treatment.

"Oh, that's all. So you always taking her side like when I came to y'all as my parents to tell you what happened to me and that I was putting the baby up for adoption then just because she threw a fit asking why wouldn't I just give the baby to her you agreed that I should even after I told you how seeing her everyday would affect my mental. The hell with my feelings your poor dried up womb golden child wanted a baby."

"You bitch all you ever did was whine about being picked on and you wonder why I am the favorite." She was talking shit but still holding her cheek where I'm sure my mother's handprint is starting to form.

"Babygirl, you know we only wanted what was best for our family. She was our blood it was only right she stay in the family." My grandmother explains their reasoning making me sick to my stomach.

"Wait so you all thought it was best for the child conceived during one of the worse moments of your child's life to stay in the family despite her vehemently expressing how it would make her feel. Damn y'all are more fucked up then I thought." Mrs. Jenkins curses my grandparents as she walks over to my mom, wrapping her up in a hug. Clearly my mother hadn't told too many people about what happened to her. My dad is standing right behind her rubbing her back. I have always loved the love and support system they have for each other.

"And y'all wonder why I moved to a different state. How could you do that to her your own daughter?" I express still completely dumbfounded.

"You will not stand in our family home and judge us as you stand holding hands with your sisters husband, God rest her soul." My grandfather attempts to shame me.

"Wow. I mean I guess I shouldn't be surprised that you're just ignoring the fact that they only got married because she didn't want him to be with me and oh yea, SHE BLACKMAILED HIM!" I shout getting pissed off at just how blatant the favoritism really is towards my aunt and Monique.

"We aren't ignoring that it's irrelevant at this point. No matter what they were married and it's wrong for you two to be together so I suggest y'all get it out of your systems and find other partners because this will not happen." My grandfather makes me laugh and he clearly is annoyed that I am not taking him seriously.

"You do not run my kids. They were meant to be before that demon child interfered. I never liked her ass even when they were just friends." Mrs. Jenkins tells my grandfather off.

"All due respect you are not a part of this family, so you have no say in what is going on here even if he is your son." Grandma has always been a damn pill but today is really taking the cake.

"But I am, and I say leave my daughter the hell alone. She doesn't have to breakup with him if she doesn't want and seeing as they have always been in love with each other I don't see it happening." Moms is not having the bullshit from my grandparents this time and I'm loving it.

"Well, if he's going to be with that tramp and seeing as Harmony isn't even his I want full custody of my granddaughter."

"You have one more time to call me out of my name you old dried up crouch goblin." I step out of Haze's arms as he's too busy laughing until it registers what she just demanded.

"You out you damn mind if you think you taking my daughter any damn where. She may not be my blood, but she is my child, I signed that muthafuckin birth certificate and so with me she stays."

"Don't worry son she doesn't want those type of problems." Mr. Jenkins steps up placing his hand on Haze's shoulder as he grabs me in his arms to calm himself but I'm past ready to whoop ha ass at this point.

"She doesn't even like yo ass like that so what makes you think a judge would give yo decrepit tales from the crypt ass custody of anything but an AARP and Medicare card." I snap because this bitch has me all the way fucked up trying to come for Harmony.

"You don't have to worry about her coming for her because if she does, I'm filing for divorce the same day." Uncle Trenton stands from the corner clearly fed up with her antics at this point.

"Ya go do what Trenton?"

"You heard me, Farah. For twenty years I have put up with your crazy antics and bullying of everyone around you that doesn't follow your every word. At first, I thought it was just built up hurt from the miscarriages but no when I sat there and thought about it you've always been so hateful. My mother god rest her soul was right about you I should have never married you, but I let my love and hope that you weren't really like that outweigh my common sense. That ends today. Sapphire baby girl please forgive me for not putting her in her place all this time with how cold she treated you and you too Trinity. So, think long and hard because I won't repeat myself." Uncle Trenton finally snaps on her, but I never judged him for it. My mom and I both run to give him a hug but with the way our men are looking at us we both walk back to them after telling Uncle Trenton, we forgive him. I never understood their dynamic anyways, he's always been so nice, warm, and giving to everyone.

"Trenton you can't be serious right now. Ya taking up for them. She was going to send her own child to be raised by strangers and this one is sleeping with our babies husband fa god sakes. Ya my husband ya supposed to be on my side." She shouts at him, and he is completely unfazed by her dramatics.

"Ok so you've clearly chosen. I want to see what judge will grant you custody at your age with no income and alone. My lawyers will be in touch. If you two ever need me though just call, I'm only done with that side of the family and I'm happy for you two." He points behind him at my aunt and grandparents then daps Haze and my dad on his way out of the office.

"Trenton come on now ya being a bit harsh aren't ya. TRENTON!" Grandpa shouts at his back since he doesn't bother to stop and just closes the door behind him.

"This is all y'all fault. I fuckin hate y'all." She screams going for my mom, but I snatch her by back by her old dry ass twenty-seven piece church grandma wig and it comes off. She turns towards me, and I swing the moment she's fully facing me catching her in the jaw. I hear the crack the moment it connects. When she falls to the floor, I jump on top of her and whisper something in her ear that makes her body still and face go pale. I just laugh as Haze lifts me off of her as she starts screaming and swinging her arms trying to hit me but as I'm being lifted off my mother jumps on her next landing a good five or six hits before my dad snatches her up too.

"Get out NOW!" Grandpa shouts jumping from his seat as grandma rushes around him to help my aunt. My mother and I smile mischievously at each other then look back at my aunt whose being helped up by my grandma and raise our legs then kick her in the chest causing both her and grandma to fly backwards into the doors but lucky for them they are tempered glass. Haze tosses me over his shoulder at this point and my dad picks my mom up bridal style to keep us from doing any more damage. Mr. and Mrs. Jenkins are killing themselves laughing and that's when I notice the whole family is staring at us from the backyard.

"Don't worry we are leaving dear old father, and you will NEVER see us again." Mr. Jenkins opens the door for us all to leave as I laugh at my grandfather's caramel face turning into a bright red tomato while trying to help grandma and aunt Farah. The moment we reach outside we are hit with a barrage of questions from cousins, aunts, and uncles and Haze has no problem addressing them quickly.

"All y'all need to know is Sapphire and I are together like we always should have been and if you have a problem with that you can get cut the fuck off like they just did."

"What my baby said." I co-sign still slung over his shoulder.

"Well, all I wanna know is why the hell no one filled me in on this. I'm your big brother Sapphire hell I use to help you two sneak around back then to avoid Mo's annoying ass before this fool married her." Garnet, my brother walks up questioning me clearly, sounding hurt. I tap Haze on the back for him to put me down.

"Chill out I'm not trying to fuck up any of your peoples for touching you wrong Phire." He warns me by gripping onto my waist with his other hand under my chin to look him in the eyes making sure I understand just how serious he is, and a shiver runs down my spine at the realization. I am definitely jumping his bones when we get back to the house.

"That's why I always liked you Haze but back to you ma'am." Garnet daps him up and these fools tickle me.

"It wasn't your fight big bro. Besides they would have never acted like they did with you in there and I wanted all their true colors once and for all."

"You know I always peeped their passive aggressive shit in the past, but I didn't realize it was this damn bad. I mean we couldn't hear everything that was said out here, but we could all tell it was heated especially when mom slapped aunty then
76

you jumped on her ass. I was out here dying laughing." I just shook my head. My big brother has always been a fool and had my back, hell between him and our parents I had nothing to worry about in college or life period.

"So, there are some things you need to know, Ma?" She nods her head and as we walk to our cars, I explain everything to him and watch as his face goes through a wide range of emotions.

"Wait that annoying ass bitch was our sister. She was bad enough as a cousin. I never understood why you took care of her ass, and she blackmailed you bro. What the hell was that serious you listened." I looked up at Haze to convey he can trust him. We walked off up the road a bit leaving the kids with their grandparents.

"I killed buddy who called himself trying to rape Phire the summer before she left for college. Her stalking ass followed me to where I did it and watched until I got rid of his ass." Garnet just rubbed his hand down his face then pulled Haze into a hug. It made my heart happy to know that the most important people to me are good with Haze and I being together.

"Thanks for handling that bro for real. I can and can't believe this one didn't tell me." He pulls me into a hug next and we stand there chatting for a while. Waving at the kids as they drove past us about to have dinner with our parents since we didn't last long at all at the function.

"I'm kinda glad all this mess came out. It's making the decision to move easier. I know a lot of people don't understand the thought process, but this shit is just too toxic for me."

"Where are you thinking about moving to?" I ask with hope he's moving close by because I seriously miss my big brother.

"Well, we just bought the house next to mom and dad." I instantly leap into his arms and kiss on his face. Now I have almost all my people in one place.

Chapter Eight

Hazekiel "Haze" Jenkins

That weekend was just as draining emotionally as I thought it would be. I did release some stress pulling up on Malakhi's bitch ass, he should really up the security on his place because it was way too easy to break into his home and wake him out of his sleep with my gun pointing at his temple. I just needed to remind his now broke ass that there was no leeching off my woman so, after a couple attitude adjustment hits and him pissing on himself I felt he got the message. Today we are all packing up to head to Kissimmee, FL for Harmony's birthday vacation. She and I were both sad seeing Sapphire and the kids get on the plane again leaving us here, but I have another surprise for my family once we get there. I end up being able to talk Sapphire into letting me pay for half of the trip at least since my parents, her parents, and her brother and his wife and kids are coming as well. Sapphire was able to find a large enough Airbnb to fit us all with room to spare thankfully.

"Alright baby grandma and grandpa just pulled up outside we need to go." I shout from downstairs in the kitchen. I hear as she zooms through the second floor and comes flying down the stairs like a bat out of hell.

"Girl slow down before we end up spending your birthday in the ER instead Disney." I scold her while grabbing our bags to head outside to the truck. I double check to make sure the alarm is set, and everything is locked up then switch spots with my dad as the driver as I usually do. The ride to the airport is filled with excited questions from my birthday girl, I still can't believe she's turning sixteen. She's growing up too fast, but I can't wait to see what a blend of Sapphire and I will look like. I plan on talking to her sooner or later about me reversing my vasectomy, hopefully it can be but if not, my doctor made sure that I stored at least two vials of my sperm just in case. It was a shocker that they even performed the procedure back then anyways, but I guess my story of not wanting to possibly die in war and leave a kid behind without me helped my case. Sometimes I wish back then I had the balls to challenge Monique about what she knew but I learn things happen for a reason plus as mature as I thought I was it was way too big of a risk to take. I've been in my thoughts so long that the darn flight is getting ready to land. Sapphire, her parents and the kids flight was earlier this morning, we took the afternoon flight since I'm still playing along that I'm going into work. While my parents and Harmony get our bags I go and retrieve our rental bus since it's so many of us. Garnet and his family should be here tomorrow. By the time I pull up to the curb they are all out waiting and ready to load up. Sapphire and the kids are waiting for us on the large front porch of the Airbnb. I looked at the photos she sent but they truly did not do this place justice. It's over four thousand square feet, two stories, six bedrooms, eight bathrooms, a large attic with a game room, a movie theater on the first floor, large eat in kitchen, and it has a decent yard with a pool. Hopping out the van, the girls rush each other, and I hear Destiny say Dontrell was being mean to her, which means now I need to have a talk with my boy if it persists.

"Hmm hi there my beauty. How is it possible you look sexier every time I see you woman?" I groan pulling her into me and leaning down to give her a kiss.

"Not sure but I know I haven't liked only seeing you a few times over the past couple months." She expresses and I share the same sentiment. Not having her in my arms every night these past two months has been torture to put it mildly.

"I know baby, I am working on somethings to have us together as a family real soon. You trust me, don't you?" I question as I'm caressing her cheek, and my parents walk past rubbing her shoulder as they do.

"With my life you know that."

"Then trust I'm working on it." She nods her head and pouts her lips for a kiss that I happily give her. We all get settled in our rooms and tonight we all decide on take out, especially since the kids want to chill in the game room by themselves, which leaves us adults to ourselves. While awaiting the food I can't help but slide in a quickie with my woman as we shower.

"Damn you always so warm and gushy baby." I moan into her ear after smacking her on the ass. That shower was supposed to be quick, but I am going to take every chance at tasting and/or filling her pussy with my seed.

"You make it that way, but don't you start, our parents are waiting on us the food got here ten minutes ago." She turns in my arms, smacking me on the chest to move. I decide to move and finish with our hygiene so we can go eat.

"Well, it's about time you two got down here I'm starving." My dad expresses making me laugh and Sapphire blush.

"Leave them alone Azaiel they have a lot of time to make up for." My mother scolds him popping him on his large chest with her small hands, I doubt it even registered to him. My father is definitely where I get my huge body frame from and still mostly muscle pops is truly the blueprint. Pops is retired military as well but he said he never believed in fighting for this country, it doesn't like us anyway, but he did it to learn the skills they taught and bring them back to our family, which made me do the same but we decided that was it for our family members going to war. I have been teaching Harmony some of what I learned and now I have Dontrell and Destiny to teach along with my soon to be wife.

"Where'd you go babe?" Sapphire whispers to me while squeezing my thigh.

"To our wedding day." I lean over to whisper in her ear then I plant a kiss behind her ear and if her mocha colored skin was light you could see her cheeks turn red, but I feel the warmth that just spread through her body.

"You two are so cute together." Mrs. Bentley says.

"True love looks good on our babies doesn't it." My mom adds and I can't help but smile. We talk about everything and nothing long after we finish dinner and move to the open floor plan family room off the dining room. We all retire to our rooms sometime after ten pm. Sapphire and I are lying in bed with her between my legs as her head rests on my chest and I run my hands through her soft thick curls. As tired as I am, something has been nagging at me about the fight at her grandparents and I can't hold it any longer.

"Babe, I need you to tell me something and keep in mind we've agreed complete honesty and never to judge but I need to know to protect you and our family."

"I have a feeling I know what's this about so go ahead and ask." She rolls over, crossing her arms on my chest and then resting her chin on them looking me in the eyes giving me her full attention.

"What did you say to your aunt at your grandparents that made her react like that?"

"I told her it wasn't the cancer that killed her precious Monique and to chill before God answers the call early to meet her maker too." She confesses with a calm straight face and if I didn't know before I know now, I love and will be marrying this damn woman sooner rather than later. To know she was the one that set me free from the hell I was living in with that demon of a woman makes a nigga heart smile.

"So, you freed me from that crazy bitch but wait how though?" I remember them not requesting an autopsy because they said she looked like she died in her sleep.

"I was switching out her chemo pills, not all of them just enough for them to think it just wasn't working then used thallium to poison her ass the remaining time since she wasn't dying quick enough." I am glad we have the music playing through the room speakers so even if someone was trying to listen, they couldn't understand a word.

"Did you make sure to cover your tracks?"

"Yes, I made sure she took all the fake chemo pills, and the thallium is untraceable at this point, and I ordered it off the dark web so no trace. If she would have just left me alone and stop being such a bitch, she might've continued to live but I did want you as well subconsciously so, I probably would've still did it." She explains as if she is giving someone a cookie recipe and I love it.

"Ok perfect. Thank you, baby." I pull her close to me planting a kiss on her soft pillowy lips and she places her hands on either side of my face deepening the kiss and I moan as our tongues enter a sensual dance.

"Get on this dick woman." I command but then a knock comes at the door.

"Ugghhh, come in." I groan as we fix ourselves under the covers.

"Daddy, Ma grandma said she's taking me away because daddy isn't my daddy!" Harmony rushes in screaming and crying. Sapphire and I both hop up from the bed to grab her in our arms, but she gets to her first and I just rub her back to calm her down.

"Is it true daddy?"

"Your grandmother isn't taking you anywhere and I am your dad even if not by blood. I was going to tell you but didn't want to on your birthday Babygirl I'm so sorry." I pull her into my arms, and she comes resting her head on my chest.

"Wait did mom cheat on you to have me and that's why y'all didn't get along like you and ma do?" She questions me standing up right looking between the two of us and Sapphire gives me the look to tell her the truth.

"Sit down for me baby there are some things we need to tell you." She sits between us on the bed, and I explain to her with the cliff notes of how things happened minus the details of the extortion and her mother being a hoe therefore not knowing who the father actually is.

"Ok that's all well and good but what about grandma taking me from you plus forbidding me any contact with you ma?" She looks over to Sapphire with concern written all over her face.

"Yo grandma ain't taking shit and I can guarantee that Harmony." I see murder in my woman's eyes when she declares and this one time I may have to steer her a different way for the sake of Harmony. Well at least at first but she doesn't get the memo quick I'll drop her ass at the bottom of my grandparent's lake with the rest of the idiots that thought it was smart to get in between my family.

"She's right your grandmother will not be taking you anywhere, now go get ready for bed we have a day loaded with fun tomorrow." I instruct her rubbing the top of her head that's covered with a silk scarf. She gives us both a kiss on the cheek and hugs then dash out the room as quickly as she came in but happier now.

"My Phire not this time well at least not right off the bat, let's do this the sensible way first, ok?" I turn her by the chin to look at me so I can see if she agrees or not.

"Fine but she can always have a heart attack, not like it would be too suspicious have you seen her medical records she really should take better care of herself." She grins.

"I always knew you were one of a kind, but I love how devious you can get. It's very... very... very sexy." I express lifting her from the bed, placing her on my lap, and she instinctively wraps her legs around me.

"Now where were we." She lifts up, freeing my dick from my basketball shorts, and slowly lowers herself until I'm hitting the back of her pussy.

"Ride yo dick my thick ass cowgirl." She pauses for a moment like I just said something she's heard. She rides me until I release every bit of my nut deep into her pussy. I wish I would have gotten my vasectomy reversed already cause she would have definitely gotten pregnant tonight. The next few days are filled with laughter, roller coasters, great food, and water parks, which is just want I wanted. Today we are chilling outside by the pool with us men outside on the grill and the ladies inside cooking up the sides while the kids swim. The ladies start coming out with trays of sides making my stomach growl but thankfully we are just putting the last slab of ribs and steaks in the pan the kids ate the jumbo grilled shrimps in between swims.

"Alright kids come on and let's eat. Y'all can get back in the pool afterwards if you want." I direct and they all come sliding to the large dining table on the patio. We say grace and everyone dugs in. Since today was actually Harmony's birthday Sapphire goes into the house to get her birthday cake.

"I wanna say happppyyyy birthday to youuu, happppyyyy birthdayyy to you, I wanna say happppyyyy birthdayyy to you, to youuu, I wanna say happppyyyy birthdayyy to you Now close your eyes and make a wish, Now close your eyes and make a wish." We all sing and clap as Sapphire sits the cake down in front of her. She has the biggest smile on her face making the plan Sapphire and I came up with just that much more important to put in place. Harmony closes her eyes to make her wish then blows out her candles as we cheer. Our parents took out their cameras snapping pictures as Sapphire and I stand to each side of her taking a finger of frosting tapping it on her nose and cheek. We sit laughing and eating cake until it is time to bring out the gifts.

"Ok Babygirl, I want you to open this one now." I give her the box as the last thing to open. She is confused seeing the stack of papers at first then she begins to read them.

"Wait daddy is this what I think it is, like for real for real!" She shouts jumping from her seat and into my arms as I am seated facing her.

"Well fill us all in why don't cha." My mom requests looking between a happy crying Harmony and me.

"Daddy is retired, and he bought some land near Ma." She shouts excitedly, doing her happy dance bouncing on her tippy toes and as it registers to everyone at the table it erupts in congratulations. After our parents give me hugs and congratulations, I grab my woman because her face looks sour for some reason.

"What's wrong baby? I thought you'd be happy about all this."

"I am it's just going to take so long to build a house for all of us to fit in and you'll still be in Georgia." She pouts and I laugh a little making her hit me in the chest as she gets mad.

"Baby we're not staying in Georgia until we finish building our home, we are moving in with y'all. I've already put in the school transfer papers for Harmony." She tippy toes to wrap her arms around my neck and gives me a kiss as I instinctively wrap my arms around her waist lifting her off the ground.

"How could you ever think I would want to be away from you that damn long baby?" She just shrugs her shoulders, and I shake my head at her putting her down. We walk back to the family and continue the celebration after we let the kids know we are moving in together.

"Wait you bought the piece of land I wanted bro. I had to get the one next to it." Garnet says as he looks over the land papers.

"Wait for real!?" Sapphire questions looking over at him.

"Yup looks like we will be neighbors lil sis." This couldn't be more perfect if I planned it myself. The kids go back to swimming after a while, and we light up the fire pit and the mosquito lanterns to keep warm and them darn things from trying to eat us alive. The rest of the week goes by so quickly with all the fun we are having. We are back home now and trying to pack up which is easier than I thought it would be since deciding to let Sapphire organize everything. Garnet and I are just the muscles. I decided not to sell the house since it's been in my family for so long, so I have renters moving in at the beginning of next month. While we are packing, I hear the ring doorbell going off, so I check the camera and notice a man at the door with an envelope in his hands, so I go answer the door.

"Hazekiel Jenkins?"

"Yes."

"You have been served." He says handing me the large yellow envelope and turns to leave. I close the door and damn near walk right into Sapphire who is coming to check who was at the door.

"Sorry baby." I say grabbing her by the waist and kissing her forehead as I'm walking around her to see what I have just been served with.

"Did that guy just say you've been served? It better not be what I think it is." She questions but more to herself than me actually.

"It is your aunt is filing for custody of Harmony on the grounds I'm not her father and child endangerment due to me dating the person who killed her daughter." I sum up what the petition section says.

"You got to be fucking kidding me? I knew I should've- "

"I thought you said she couldn't take me and ma did you really kill mommy." Harmony shouts from the steps with so much hurt in her voice.

"Come here Harmony." She shakes her head no as tears start to form in the corners of her eyes, but she finally decides to come down when I tell her again.

"Look Babygirl this is just an attempt on her part she has no grounds to actually take you from me. I will get my lawyers on it asap I promise." I declare.

"And no baby I did not kill your mother she died from cancer. Your grandmother is only saying these things to hurt us and take you, but we won't let her, ok?" She nods her head as Sapphire caresses her cheek looking at her in the eyes. I can tell it hurt her to lie but there is no way we can tell her the truth of how her mother died. We share a look deciding to put our plan into effect since she wants to play with fire. I step away calling my lawyer who thankfully works at a law firm that includes family lawyers which the one he set me up with is one of the best in the state.

"How the hell did she get this expedited so quick?" Sapphire questions after Harmony goes back upstairs to finish packing her room up.

"She must have found out about us moving. It's all good I have a meeting with the family lawyer in two days. Hey don't do that this changes nothing. We are still packing this place up and moving in with you and the kids." I reassure her as I see the worry start to cross her eyes. She gives me a weak smile, but I'm not worried about it because she will be fully happy soon enough. We finish packing the pod yesterday and it's on the road headed to my woman. I sent her and the kids home this morning while I manage this bullshit custody case. Looking at myself in the shiny elevator walls I must say ya boy cleans up nice. I decided on one of my tailored navy blue dress pants and pastel pink polo with tan Steve Madden dress shoes. My woman gave me an early birthday gift a gold navy blue face watch with diamonds where the numbers would be made by this Black owned company, and she has the matching women's version. The elevator dings ending my admiration of myself and I make the first left knocking on the office door for my new lawyer.

"Come in."

"Ah Mr. Jenkins nice to meet you." Drew Scales greets standing then walking from behind his desk to shake my hand then walks back taking his seat again. I take the seat in front of his desk, and we get down to business.

"Ok so let me make sure I have all this correct. You were blackmailed by the mother of the child, who has now passed on from cancer, she didn't even know who the child's biological father is, and the only reason any of this came about is because you are now with the cousin of the child's mother which is her godmother, and you all are moving in together. You are of course the only father she knows and on the birth certificate along with all other paperwork. Oh, you also mentioned that the grand mother is getting a divorce from her husband because he doesn't agree with what she is doing, and he is the sole provider well was in their home?" He sums up everything I told him.

"Yes, that's all correct." I confirm.

"Well this will be open and shut really quickly unless she has evidence that Ms. Bentley committed the crime she is alleging she did, which you claim is completely false and that your daughter has expressed she does not want to live with her grandmother anyways."

"Yes, that is everything in a nutshell. Monique had been sick for a while, and we had just found out that her chemotherapy was not effective. The doctors were looking into medical trials to place her in as her cancer had progressed, so we knew the risk of her dying in between treatments. She didn't even know until their family blow out that Harmony is not biologically mines or that I never wanted to marry her daughter which is actually my woman's sister conceived during the rape of her mother." When I added that little tidbit, he broke his professional mask really quick.

"What the hell, wait explain that please." I broke it down for him as he wrote note after note is his notebook.

"Ok so this woman has some narcissistic tendencies and just blatant disregard for others including family. Well Mr. Jenkins, you have handed me a pretty easy case and I will get all paperwork submitted. When it comes to the court date you have the choice to be there, but I always recommend that my clients show for all court dates."

"Consider me there." We go over some more details and signing of paperwork then I am headed to my family. I sent my suitcase ahead with them so all I needed to do is catch my flight. As I wait at the airport for my flight to board my beautiful woman calls me.

"Hi beautiful." I answer.

"Hi baby, how did the meeting go?"

"It went well baby. I told you that I had it."

"I know babe. I can't wait until you get here. I unpacked your suitcase and put your clothes away."

"Thanks babe. They are calling for my flight I will see you soon." She says bye and I end the call. The flight is quick and calm, but I am still anxious to hurry up and get to my family. I made Sapphire stay home instead of coming back to the airport to get me and I take a rideshare. She gave me a key before I left, so I let myself in and its late afternoon at this point. The house is surprisingly quiet, so I head straight to the room I'll be sharing with my woman, and I find her asleep in bed. I walk over to give her a kiss on the lips, she stirs a bit then opens her eyes.

"Babe you're here." She smiles, pulling me in for another kiss.

"Yea I'm here baby, go on back to sleep, I'm about to shower and come take a nap with you." I direct as I give her another quick kiss then walk to jump in the shower by the time I get out she is fast asleep on the other side of the bed because she knows I like to sleep close to the door. I decide to just leave my boxers on and get into bed pulling her back into my front making my dick get hard instantly when I notice she's completely naked. I can't help but rub my hands over the smooth skin of her ass and thighs then rubbing my fingers between her lips that are already slick with her juices.

"Mmm babe." She moans reaching back to pull my head towards her and I bite down on her shoulder just enough for her to feel some slight pain as I circle her entrance before dipping two of my fingers inside her pussy. She turns her head pulling me into a slow sensual kiss and I find her g spot hitting it continuously until she's moaning in my mouth with her juices running down my fingers. I bite her bottom lip then suck it between my lips.

"Lick them clean." I demand her as I put my fingers that are soaked into her mouth. She looks at me right in my eyes as she

93

snakes her tongue around my fingers then sucks them both into her warm inviting mouth.

"Good girl." I groan into her ear as I enter her to the hilt in one swift motion while still laying behind her. I hit her g spot with three long deep strokes then get up on my knees with one of her legs between mines while holding the other in my arm at my waist.

"Oooh fuck Haze." She cries out and I look down at where we connect as she creams all over my dick.

"Look at my pretty pussy creaming all over ha dick, keep that shit coming." I demand as I lean forward placing kisses up her side as she turns to lay her back on the bed giving me full access to her large H size breast and suck her erect nipple in between my lips. In this angle I have her completely exposed and I feel like I'm hitting her cervix which she confirms.

"Shit baby you are so fucking deeeeppp." She moans as I keep stroking her into her next orgasm.

"That's my woman, you're taking this dick so fucking good. Now give me that nut baby." As if all she needed was my permission her juices begin raining down on me so much, so she coats my nuts and inner thighs.

"Fuck you're so responsive, baby." I moan smacking her on the ass and enjoying the sight of it rippling. I turn her over and she arches her back just like I like it but I push her upper body flat on the mattress then I flatten my feet on the bed in a squat position while placing my hands right above her ass and thrust as deep as her pussy will allow.

"FFUUUUUCCCKKK" She screams as I keep my pace of quick deep strokes but slow down when I feel her squirting all over my lower body. I spread her knees farther apart to continue hitting that other spot in her pussy that drives her wild.

"Keep giving me those juices Sapphire. I want it all baby. You will feel me even when you're at your desk working every day." I switch my angle up now carving my name in her side walls.

"Rub that clit my lil freak." She does as I tell her and wraps my fingers in her soft curls pulling just enough. She comes undone for me with her body trembling and I feel the tingle start at my toes then my balls tightening up which let me know my nut isn't far behind. With a few more strokes I am filling her honey pot full of my nectar.

"Shit woman." I groan after smacking her ass then kissing the same spot. I lay next to her trying to catch my breath because she makes me cum so damn hard.

"I am going to need to work in more cardio work if you keep fucking me like this Haze."

"We can get it in together. Now come on let's take a quick shower and I see you bought your own blanket." I pull her to me for a quick kiss while grabbing her ass and she moans. She thinks she is going to need more cardio but the way I want to be in this woman's skin every time I see or even hear her voice, I am going to need it more cardio and those natural herbs she wants to grow so badly. I get up from the bed and pick her up bridal style and head to the bathroom placing her on the toilet while I turn the shower on then go to remove the intimacy blanket throwing it in the laundry basket. We try to take a quick shower but my lil freak wanted to suck on her lollipop then get fucked up against the shower wall. It's been a little over a week since moving in with the love of my life along with our kids completing our family. I have been working on a surprise with our parents and kids, and we are about to reveal the surprise. Our parents as well as siblings are already setting up with the kids on the land I purchased to build our new home. My phone starts to ring through my car speakers and it's my woman right in time.

"Good evening my Phire." I answer with a smile on my face so wide my cheeks puff up with my dimples in both very prominent.

"Hi my honey bun. I just got off and I am heading to our land plot, but I still want to know what this surprise is. Can I at least get a hint?" She questions sounding impatient which I knew she would be and that's exactly why I didn't tell her about it until yesterday.

"Babe you will literally be to our land plot in twenty minutes." I reassure her.

"Fine but it better be good you know I have never been one for surprises. Well, I'm hopping on the highway babe see you in a bit."

"Drive safe, I love you."

"I love you too." She replies as I am pulling up to our land and everything looks perfect. The string lights, the tents, the flower arches, wooden tables lined with burlap runners and wildflowers mixed with sunflowers and daisy's, the few white wooden chairs with crochet back covers made by Mrs. Bentley, and the tan runner leading to the main arch.

"Wow guys this looks absolutely perfect." I express still looking at all the other details that make up the most beautiful country setting and not to mention by the time Sapphire reaches the sun will be setting right behind us adding to the ambiance.

"It really is bro. My sister is going to love this, well after she smacks you for surprising her." Garnet chuckles bumping shoulders with me. He and his family moved here last week after the closing was finalized a few days prior to their arrival. We had a family meeting to coordinate everything to my woman's liking.

"Well brother you are about to be on I hear her car pulling up. Good luck." We fist bump, then Garnet rushes off into the tent setup for everyone to change when the time comes. I swear all of a sudden, my damn palms are sweaty as hell. Nothing makes me nervous but confronting my beautiful soul in human form to ask her the most important question you can ask a woman. Her car stops next to my F150 and when she steps out the car it's like God shined down on me and granted me access to his most prized creation.

"Wow babe what is all this, it's so beautiful." She asks with the cutest doe eyed look as she looks around at everything that is set up. I gently grab her hand to pull her towards me and she's already teary-eyed.

"Sapphire, you know I have always loved you, but I knew we were meant to be together since the day you walked into Ms.

Jessie's homeroom class in seventh grade. I know most would say I was too young to know but I did and that love just grew stronger and deeper as the years went on. Then we had our first kiss sophomore year, and I felt a part of my soul click into place. I have been partially living for the past fifteen years and now that I have you back, I don't want to waste any more time." I dropped down to one knee and pulled the burgundy velvet ring box out that's been burning a hole in my pocket.

"Oh my gosh." She exclaims when I open the box to show her the oval shaped ruby surrounded by smaller diamonds on a twenty-four karat gold band. Only the best for my woman.

"You have been my wife in my head for a very long time but now I want to make it official baby. So will you do me the honor and be my-"

"YES... Yes of course I will." She falls down to her knees pulling my face into hers for a heated kiss.

"So, you know how I said I didn't want to waste anytime right?" I inquire while sliding the ring on her finger as all of our family starts coming out from the different tents dressed up to the nines, along with my church pastor I flew in yesterday.

"Aww babe." She starts to cry, and I pull her to me kissing each tear.

"So, what do you say, we getting married today?" I question and she nods her head looking at the kids who look absolutely beautiful in their floral dress and tailored tux. Our family finally reaches us and starts to hug and congratulate us.

"My wife said yes so let's get this wedding rolling." I clap my hands over my head. The ladies grab my wife and head over to their tent and walk over to mines.

Chapter Nine

Sapphire Jenkins

I am still reeling with excitement and the love I feel pouring from my man and our family. When we walk into the tent he had designated for us to change the tears really start to fall. There is a hairstylist and makeup artist and along the right side of large tent is a rack of four different wedding dresses. My man knows how I feel about even numbers because that last dress is a no for me but the other three are going to be hard to choose from.

"So, I know you like to be different, and you love my crochet work so me and your soon to be mother in law made this for you." My mother hands me the most beautiful veil I have ever seen and trust I have looked at plenty fantasizing about this very day. The veil is crocheted in this intricate diamond pattern with what looks like hundreds of Swarovski crystals in the center of each diamond. The length of it had to have taken at least a couple days along with the other design attributes because this thing would drag on the floor as I walked. I grabbed them both into my arms hugging them tightly as we all shed a few tears. Looking back at the gowns again I know exactly the one I want to wear that compliments this veil perfectly. The hairstylist did some soft loose curls after adding some clip ins to make it look fuller and I had the make artist do a light natural beat as I've never been one for wearing a lot of makeup.

"OK here's your something blue." Mrs. Jenkins hands me a powder blue garter and I lift my dress to slide it on then give her another hug.

"Your father wanted you to have this. It's your great grandmothers. It was given to her by your great grandfather as the first high priced item outside of their home of course." Mom placed the bracelet that is a combination of ruby's and diamond just like my engagement ring but you can see the age in the bracelet but it's still beautiful. I walk over to the tall mirror towards the front of the tent and my eyes instantly well up with tears.

"Awwww look at how beautiful my girl looks." Mom starts dabbing at her eyes as tears begin to fall.

"Hey... hey... hey no messing up my masterpieces. I mean you all made it easy. I've had some beautiful women as clients before but all of you are gorgeous." The makeup artist compliments us all and we thank her. I have to admit my man knows me very well from the size and cut of the dress, the style, wait did I mention it has pockets, yes girl pockets!

"Aight ladies it's time to-" Dad starts to rush us until he notices me in the corner still admiring myself in the mirror. He starts to tear up as he's walking up to me, and I turn to give him a hug which I still feel like his little girl getting a hug since he's such a large man. He has a bit of a dad bod but he and mom walk at least six miles three days out the week or go swimming so he's in shape, but he is still over six foot two and probably around two hundred pounds. I am a mere five foot five.

"Babygirl, you look like a chocolate angel. I'm so happy to be walking you down the aisle today."

"I wouldn't have anyone else do it. You have been the best dad a girl could ask for. From learning how to do my hair when mom's law career took off, then finding the perfect beautician and turning my appointment days in to a princess pamper day with going to get our nails done, facials, and cooking classes. Not to mention when I was getting bullied in elementary school for being different you took me to the gym and gave me boxing lessons yourself for months not to just be able to defend but get my confidence back with all the affirmations you would speak to me while we trained. Wait no when my grown ass developed panic attacks after trying to repress my anger for everything that Malakhi put me through you and mom both learned how to help me through them because I didn't want to take anxiety meds." We're all in tears by the time I finish expressing how my dad has been the greatest to me growing up as well as an adult. I still run to him when I need one of his King Bear hugs as he use to call them. The makeup artist touches up all of our makeup. I hear one of our other favorite songs from India Aire's album "The Truth" start to play and it brings back a memory from back during the summer before tenth grade. Mo was thankfully on vacation, so we didn't have to worry about her interrupting us. We spent the day riding the horses on his grandparents farm, having a picnic with food we stopped at the family grocery store, they had the best sandwiches, then just lay under the big red oak and listened to music watching the sunset. It was the perfect day. Destiny is the flower girl and groomsmen and bridesmaids go out next then I hear one of our favorite old schools by Freddie Jackson

"You Are My Lady" signaling for my dad and I to start down the aisle and the moment I lock eyes with my man the tears start. He mouths to me that I look beautiful while dabbing his eyes with his handkerchief. Haze looks so edible in his navy blue and black tailored tux with a fresh tape and waves looking sickening per usual. The suit might've been tailored but his muscles are still prominent from the arms down. I can't wait to see that round lil booty of his.

"Who gives this woman away?" The pastor inquires.

"I do. I love you so much Babygirl and you young man I expect you to protect my princess with your life." Dad states placing my hand in Haze's who helps me up the one step even though it wasn't needed since I went with the studded white cowgirl boots, he picked out for me as a possible shoe. Haze nods his acknowledgment to my father and as I stand in looking up into his beautiful honey brown eyes, I see the intensity in which he will protect me.

"We are gathered here to honor and celebrate the love shared between these two people, as they come together to start their new life with a solemn vow. May your love be a source of joy, a foundation of strength, and a testament to the enduring power of commitment. Now these two beautiful souls wanted to say a few words." Haze nods towards me to go first.

"Haze, you've always held my heart—from laughter as kids to our secret rendezvous as teenagers then to adulthood. Life has given us a second chance, and I vow to never let anyone come between us again. You're my one true love, my home, my forever. I choose you, now and always, with every heartbeat." I finish with Haze using his thumb to wipe at my tears as I do the same for his and place his titanium band on him.

"Sapphire, losing you was like losing the sun—everything dimmed and placed me on autopilot. I ached for your voice, your smile, us. I fought through the dark for this moment, for you. Protecting you is second nature for me, and I will do it until my last breath. You are my peace, my fire, my forever. I love you—always have, always will." This man has me in full blown tears, and he kisses everyone that falls then takes off my engagement ring placing my wedding band and engagement ring back on.

"Now that was beautiful. May the love you two share today be a source of strength and comfort for all the years to come. Go now, and may God bless you both." He announces and Haze has be wrapped in his arms planting a soul sucking knee buckling kiss. When he licks my lips, I open for him allowing our tongues to do their own tango and I place my hands on either side of his face while his hand grip my hips pulling me closer.

"Hmmm." Our parents clear their throats as the kids giggle and our silly siblings are whistling. We laugh as we part turning to everyone and smiling. The night could not have gone any better had I planned it myself. After one last kiss from my husband I strut over to my tent to change into this beautiful white cocktail dress that also has pockets, lace, and small crystals on the skirt part. Joining my husband in our thrown like chairs.

"How did I do baby?" Haze questions leaning over to speak into my ear.

"This is absolutely perfect Haze. You thought of everything and nothing is over the top, country quaint, and warm." I kiss him on the cheek, and he squeezes my thigh causing me to bite into my bottom lip. Our parents each get up to speak along with his brother and Shamara, my brother's wife, who was my maid of honor. I am sitting in a chair in the middle of the tent with my man strutting over to me then he kneels taking my left leg and placing it on his shoulder after taking off my boot. I am so glad we already did the daddy daughter dance, and they left with the kids because this man just grabbed my garter with his teeth as "Sexual Healing" by Al Green plays in the background. Every part of my body is heating up with each pull downwards. When he gets it off, he pulls me to the edge of the seat and plants kisses up my leg then bites on my inner thigh making me wet the seat of my thong immediately. Before I can wrap my head around what is about to happen I hear moaning from my right and turning my head to look I can partially make out in the dim light a woman sitting on top of the table with her legs spread wide but before I can tell who it is I feel heat from Haze's mouth then his tongue.

"Shit babe! We... We're in the middle of... of the room." I moan as he truly starts his assault on my pussy after moving my panties to the side. He flattens his tongue then licks me from my entrance to my clit, flicking it a few time before sucking it between his lips, and circling it with his tongue. I grab the back of his head pushing him further into my pussy as he dips his tongue into my pussy circling against my walls.

"Sh... shiiiit... shiit." I stutter trying to catch my breath as I hear more moaning around me and then my orgasm sneaks up on me so hard my vision goes hazy and my toes lockup.

"Your pussy will forever be my favorite meal and dessert." He moans as he licks his lips, and I pull him in for a wet kiss tasting myself on his tongue. I finally get to look around and realize it is a full blown orgy going on around us from our brothers to some of Haze's army buddies with their wives. Hell, one of the wives or girlfriends are taking two of them at the same time, one is fucking her throat while the other is deep in her guts.

"Babe is there really an orgy going on at our wedding reception?" I ask as Haze picks me up and I wrap my legs around his waist as he carries me out of the tent after cleaning me up.

"Well, this should be a wedding night to remember, huh?"

"Memorable for sure." I shiver as the night air hits my bare legs only. Thankfully Haze wrapped his jacket around me before we left the tent.

"Don't worry baby we are going just over here." He points with his head, and I lay my head on his shoulder as my arms are wrapped around his neck. We walk for about five more minutes then I lift my head to this beautiful large trailer with a huge porch that has a swing. I can't wait to drink some tea and read a book on it. The lights around it are clearly motion activated since they weren't on before we got close.

"Oh my gosh babe it's beautiful."

"It's only temporary. I figured we can come here when we want to get away or keep an eye on the contractors as they build our home." He explains as he's opening the screen then front door. I unwrap myself from him once we're inside admiring the open floor plan. I can literally see the kitchen living room and dining room from the front door, but it wasn't a small space at all. This home has to be at least two thousand square feet walking further into the living. I notice a master suite to the right then what looks like a decent size office to the left, another sitting room, across from what I can tell looks like the laundry room. He has it fully furnished with very comfy but modern style furniture.

"This is really nice babe. How many bedrooms are in here and please tell me we are spending our honeymoon here?" I question while admiring the large island.

"It's four bedrooms and three bathrooms. You know Jr has a plumbing company, so he came out with his crew before it was delivered to bring the plumbing from the road here. There is a large solar panel generator outside for the power, so yes if you are ok with this being our first honeymoon spot." He replies grabbing me by the waist and lifting me on top of the island.

"Sir what do you mean by first honeymoon spot?"

"You really think this is all I am doing after finally getting the woman I have loved for most of my life? This is just the beginning and only due to the fact we have court next week with Mo's crazy as auntie mother."

"Hahaha you but babe you bought land, paid for the contractors, paid and planned a beautiful wedding, and bought all this. You've done more than enough. I don't want us going into any kind of debt anyways."

"Baby, do you think I would ever put you in the position to struggle or need or want for any damn thing? I know it's the overthinking part of your brain kicking in so I won't take offense this time and to ease your mind read over this and sign." He explains and I feel a bit bad about insinuating that he's doesn't know how to manage his money but what I wasn't expecting is for him to pull out a thick folder from one of the drawers labeled finances and estate planning. Thumbing through the folder as he walks over to the fridge grabbing a bottle of wine then two glasses from the cabinet next to it. I almost drop the entire folder when I reach a page labeled estate estimated value of forty million dollars.

"Close ya mouth before I put something in it woman. I told you before I made some investments what I didn't say was that even before those investments my parents made some of the same back when we were kids and hit really big. They both reinvested half then put the other half in a trust for Jr and I that earned a sizable amount of interest and by the time we inherited it on our twenty fifth birthday it had over ten million apiece. You know what Jr did with his and a part of what I did with mine, which is the grocery store, but I have two others, plus six rental properties. I said all that to say this Sapphire you and our kids current as well as future have absolutely nothing to worry about financially. Hell, if you want you can quit your job, don't even start I know you wouldn't." This man continues to leave me flabbergasted at how much thought he has put into us being together and how strategic he is with his money which is sexy within itself.

"I'm sorry for doubting you babe. I am still getting use to the grown-up version of you."

"It's all good baby. My job is to show you that our family is safe, and I shall do that. Now what do you think about trying out this large, jetted soaker tub we have?"

"Sounds good to me." He lifts me off the island then grabs the bottle of wine I can't even pronounce but it tastes good. When we enter the master suite, I notice it has a sitting area before the actual room then two large walk-in closets in the hallway. We enter the spacious room and the first thing I see is the cherry wood California king size four poster bed right in the middle covered in deep burgundy silk and I mean real silk sheets and a velvety soft blanket folded at the foot. I can't wait to snuggle up with my husband. He leaves me to explore the room while he gets the shower and tub going. I know I am a little extra, but I prefer to shower before I soak in the tub otherwise, I feel like I'm soaking in my dirt, yuck.

"Sapphire the showers ready baby." I sashay my way back to the bathroom and am greeted by my dream bathroom. It has dark blue cabinets, separate sinks, large soaker tub, and even larger shower that has two rain shower heads then two detachable heads on either side.

"I take it I remembered everything correctly my love?" He inquires wrapping me up in his muscular arms.

"Yes, down to the all gold fixtures." I lean my head back for a kiss that he obliges. We strip down and hop in the shower doing a good wash then in the tub we went.

"This feels amazing and are these my bubbles?" I ask him as I slide in the front of him.

"Not the exact bottle from the house but I did buy all the same hygiene stuff you use at home and some new stuff mama Bentley recommended for you."

"Wait you went shopping with my mom?"

"Yes, we had a mother and son day. My mom even came with us. It was really nice actually. I always knew she was the sweetest but experiencing her now. I see why you turned out so great well besides Pops Bentley that man is the truth." He explains as he massages my shoulders.

"So, did you have a father son day with my dad too?"

"I did. Our day was a bit different him and my dad worked out here with me and my brothers team. We also worked on this house together once it was delivered last week. Even helped me with the finishing touches of our bed and dressers."

"Babe, you built our bedroom furniture?" I question turning my upper body to slightly face him in complete shock.

"I did. It has become my favorite piece that I have made to date." I pull him in for a quick kiss that quickly turns heated and before I can think twice, I am turned completely around then sliding down his thick long dick. It takes my breath away the moment he fills me to the hilt.

"Shit baby." He hisses grabbing my hips and I feel his foot twitch then I hear the water start to drain. That man fucks me in every room of this house and waking up this morning I feel it in every part of my body. I swear my pussy is swollen he fucked me so damn good; I had to sleep with my damn legs open.

"There's my sleeping beauty." Haze greets me with a tray of food and drinks. I sit up so he can place it in front of me and then gives me a kiss.

"Babe this all smells amazing and clearly my stomach agrees." I giggle as my stomach growls so damn loudly if I wasn't married to this hunk of a man I might've been embarrassed. He laughs at me before walking out to grab his own tray.

"Sorry for not feeding you last night baby. It being our wedding night kinda woke up something in me." He's actually sorry about it this man's level of affection and care for knows no bounds.

"Haze, I appreciate you making us breakfast and last night well the entire day was mind blowing. Especially the session in the kitchen at the island with the butt plug while I signed the estate and investment paperwork." I give him a side eye while placing a piece of the soft with just enough crisp around the edges and perfectly sweet French toast he made into my mouth.

"You keep looking at me like that I won't let the lil kitty of yours rest at all today." He warns me in between bites of his own food. We eat in silence for the rest of our morning with just stolen glances or gentle brushes against the shoulder. I was feeling a bit bubbly after he fed me all those mimosas during breakfast. After a good shower he packs a go bag while I was getting dressed in his Nike basketball shorts but one of my tank tops, and a pair of sneakers he bought me. This man thinks of everything I swear.

"So how many acres is it exactly?" I ask as we walk hand in hand across our property.

"It's sixty acres to be exact and your brother's property starts about ten acres back that way." He points out to the left of our land, but we seem to be walking towards the woodsy area which looks burnt.

"Aww babe what happen to the grass and some of the trees they look burnt up?" I ask.

"Now how did my country girl forget one of the main techniques we use to ward off wildlife like snakes and other critters." He pokes me in the side and it all clicks.

"That's right. Well, it has been a while since I've been on a large plot of land. So, that means it's snake free right?" I question looking down as we step past the perimeter of the wood area.

"Yes, part of what we did after putting out the fire we went through most of the wooded area with some snake away and something for the other bugs." I tiptoe to kiss him on the cheek, but he lets my hand go which makes me pout and miss his touch just that fast.

"Baby I want to try something with you which is going to require you to really trust me, do you?" Haze questions standing behind me and rubbing my shoulders.

"I trust you with everything babe and I think I know what you want to try."

"What do I want Sapphire, say it." He says low in my ear with his husky voice.

"I'm your prey and you are the predator that's going to chase me through the woods then fuck me." I say just above a whisper as my heart starts to race with just the thought of what he may do.

"Yes, are you going be a good Lil prey for me Sapphire?" He growls low in my ear and I nod my response which was clearly my first mistake because I feel something sharp poke me in the side.

"Always use your words baby. Now here's how it is going to go, I will give you a fifteen second head start, and then every time I catch you, I will cut a piece of clothing off and once I cut the last piece, I fuck you wherever we are, understand?" He brings his arm up and over my chest then I feel a sharp blade Glide against my breast causing my nipples to harden instantly.

"Yes sir." I moan leaning my head back on his chest.

"Good girl now... run." He whispers in my ear then releases me and I take off with no objective in sight.

Chapter Ten

Hazekiel "Haze" Jenkins

My dick bricked up at the sight of my wife's juicy ass bouncing as she takes off running into the woods to play along with my sick little game.

"Fifteen, fourteen, thirteen, twelve, eleven, ten, nine, eight, seven, six, five, four, three, two, and one. Ready or not her I come." I count down loudly as I hear her footsteps getting farther away. I take a few steps to listen for which way she is headed. The moment I catch her steps to my left I take off in that direction and easily catch up to her, but I stay hidden behind a tree watching her. She is trying her hardest to be quiet, listening out for my movements, and looking around carefully. Sapphire is going to make this a very fun game.

"Shit." She curses after mis stepping and breaking a twig. I take my chance to pounce on her in that moment of frustration wrapping my arms around then taking the blade I've been holding running it down the middle of the thin fabric she calls a shirt.

"Uhmm hi there beautiful." Growling low in her ear and licking the sweat off her neck.

"Get off mee." She fights against my hold, elbowing me in the side then darting through the trees. She just made this better than I could have ever imagined. With a throaty growl I take off after my soul in human form. I narrowly dodge a branch she throws at me, I dart around another tree and snatch her towards me by her long ponytail.

"Ouch shit." She shouts trying to snatch away from me still fighting.

"Stay still my beauty or you might get nicked by the knife." I warn her before sliding the knife over the knot in the tied straps on my basketball shorts and they fall to the ground. She moans rubbing against my lower body and I notice she doesn't have any underwear on. I didn't think my dick could get any harder than it already is but fuck was it standing like a steel pipe poking her in the back.

"You keep rubbing up on me like that I'm going to say fuck the rules and bend you over right here." I groan into her ear about to lose my grip on the game. She does something that makes me love the shit out of her even more, she turns her head and sinks her teeth into my arm then she takes off again.

"Ugghhh I love you woman!" I shout into the trees at her back. This time it takes me a minute to find her and this time her lovely scent gives her away but this time I don't grab her instantly, I sneak up behind the tree she's hiding behind and I slice the back of one strap then quickly do the other. The moment the shock kicks in I snatch off my bookbag I've been carrying off and snatch her up off the ground then push her up against the tree.

"All out of clothing there my beautiful wife, hmmm you know what that means." A growl releases deep in my chest as I use my other hand to loosen the knot in my basketball shorts then ramming my long hard steel in straight to the hilt.

"Fuuuckkk." She screams, slaps me, then pulls me in for a heated kiss. I fuck her roughly against the tree glad the tree she picked has no rough bark on it otherwise my babies back would be scarred.

"Sh... shhii...shiiittt." She moans loudly gushing all over my dick. I'm not far behind her until I hear footsteps in the distance. We are a good quarter mic in but I've been trained to hear the slightest disturbance.

"Dad I don't think she's screaming from that type of pain, let's just wait for them at the house." I hear Garnet trying to reason with their father, but Sapphire is still enjoying the sex since I haven't stopped stroking this wet, warm, and tight pussy of hers.

"Wait, ah mannnn y'all nasty." Pops Bentley shouts right as I bite down on her shoulder and cum.

"Oh, shut up Gemini it's not like we haven't had sex outside before hell plenty of times." Mama Bentley scolds him, and Sapphire finally hears them as she comes down from her back to back orgasm. I slowly slid out of her letting her down at the same time and can't help but chuckle at her mother's comment.

"They are so gross, they can't see us can they, oh shit all my clothes." She begins to panic but I walk around the tree to grab the bookbag I was carrying to grab the extra clothes I packed.

"Here baby." I hand them to her and kiss her on the forehead, shaking out my shorts and putting them back on.

"Thanks babe you think of everything I swear." She tip toes to give me a quick kiss then starts to put on her clothes.

"Babe don't worry they are heading back to the house." I reassure her by rubbing her cheek with my thumb now that she is fully dressed.

"This was amazing Sapphire. I really never thought I would be able to live out this fantasy with you, thanks for not being freaked out." I give her another kiss then grab her hand in mine, and we start to walk back towards the open yard.

"Haze, I loved every bit of what we just did. It's been something I wanted to try since learning it was a kink, and I want to do it again without being interrupted but next time you're the prey big man." She taps me on the chest, and I chuckle.

"Whatever you want my love." I kiss her hand that I am holding, and we continue the walk to join our family at the house for dinner. We spent our week exploring other kinks as well as building my wives dream garden. Her and Garnets wife had him, our fathers, and me out for three days straight building raised garden beds, then filling then the over two thousand dollars' worth of soil she bought that she and not me complained about the cost. It became a whole family event with the kids and moms joining in, we even brought out the grill for some ribs, hot dogs and burgers. I would do all that labor again just to see the smile on my wife's face or the giddy dance she did once all the seeds and pre grown trees were planted exactly where they wanted. Today is our court date, we decided the kids would stay with her parents while mines came with us for support.

"Good morning Mr. Jenkins and-"Mr. Scales greets us then turns to my wife staring a little too damn hard for my liking. He's going to end up in zip lock bags if he doesn't move his

117

eyes elsewhere, I haven't had to dismember a body in a very long time but hey they say muscle memories is real.

"That is my wife Sapphire Jenkins, and it would be in your best interest to stop staring so hard." I warn him while eyeing him with a scowl on my face and tapping my fingers against Sapphire's waist.

"I apologize Mr. Jenkins. They should be calling us in any second." He apologizes, greets my parents, then proceeds to look at his phone like he just received a message to busy himself. Just like he said they called us to come in and while we are sitting Mo's mother comes in with her lawyer giving us the evil eye and I almost burst into laughter when I notice Sapphire holding up her ring finger. My woman is so petty and so is my mother because she stuck up the middle finger. My dad was holding in his laughter too but the big smile and his broad shoulders bouncing gave him away. The court officer did his whole spiel and then the judge asked the lawyer the reason for the petition.

"Your honor my client is filling for full custody of her grandchild due to Mr. Jenkins not being the biological father of said grandchild." Her lawyer stands to reply.

"Ok I see here that the daughter has been deceased for around eight years now and his name is the name on the child's birth certificate as well as they were married at the time of her death. So, what is the true reason for this petition and don't waste my time?" The judge reiterated the question with the facts, and I can tell I am going to like him already. The lawyer looks down at her, I guess to get confirmation about the mess he was about to say next.

"Your honor she recently found out that her granddaughter is not biologically Mr. Jenkins. She also believes that the woman that Mr. Jenkins is in court with today, who also is her niece, is responsible for the death of her daughter and may be a danger to her grandchild." The lawyer drops the bombshell I was not expecting for her dumb ass to put out in the court and now I wish I would have listened to my wife and just killed this bitch.

"Your honor I object they have absolutely no proof my clients wife is any danger to the child or these false allegations." My lawyers jump up to defend us.

"You sit and you speak quickly because these are serious allegations." The judge orders.

"Yes, your honor. The only reason we are here today is due to these simple facts the plaintiff is upset that my client has remarried to her daughter's cousin, who is actually her sister, after it being revealed that Mr. Jenkins was blackmailed into marrying the plaintiff's daughter and claiming his daughter to begin with. We have the letter in her deceased daughters handwriting proving such and as far as my clients wife being a danger to his daughter, I highly doubt that the mother would have made her the god mother if she believed she would harm her, which she has no history in the sixteen years she's been in her life of doing. Finally, she has no current income, will be moving back in with her parents due to the mess divorce she is currently going through that will be putting the house she currently resides in for sale, and we have video of my client's daughter with a licensed child psychologist, who is here with us today, giving her statement as to why she wants to stay with the two people she considers her parents." Mr. Scale's finishes then hands the letter we edited to replace certain facts, the video of my baby girl, and the statement from Mama Bentley about the nature of how Monique became her daughter the judge requested. When I look over to Mo's mom and she has this shit face pissed off look.

"Recess for one hour while I review the evidence provided." He slams his gavel, we all stand, and then leave.

"You two ain't shit. How could you marry this huzzy? I really thought so much better of you Hazekiel." She shouts the moment we all sit on one of the benches outside the courtroom.

"Don't either of you dare I got this delulu having ass bitch." Ma jumps up in her face real fast and I notice the fear slide across her eyes the moment she is close.

"Now let me tell yo trifling ass something. I put up with your miserable ass the entire time my child was held captive by your witch of a daughter and now that he his finally at peace and happy with his true wife I will not let you ruin it. So, take you lopsided wig, depends draws wearing, slough footed, Pomeranian face ass on your side of the hallway before we have a serious coming to Jesus moment." Oh, that was it for all of us even our lawyers snickered while we were bent over grabbing our stomachs, we were laughing so hard. She took the hint and turned to walk off with a look of true embarrassment, but she deserved so much more, and she would get it sooner than she may have thought. We talked amongst ourselves and grabbed a few things to snack on since we already had lunch reservations. Before we know it the hour has past and we are being called back into the courtroom. Once seated the judge starts in.

"First Mr. Jenkins thank you for you service. I was able to speak with your commanding officer and he sang your praises. Also, congratulations on being newly retired. Now to you Mrs. Murphy I am denying you full custody of the child in question Harmony Jenkins. I am ordering six months at minimum of therapy before any further visits with her. I read the letters from your sister, watched the video of your granddaughter, and I spoke with your soon to be ex-husband and I have concluded you are very disturbed woman. Once you have completed your court ordered therapy you will then have supervised visits only with the child until she is eighteen years of age and can decide whether she wants to continue a relationship. I here so order." He slams his gavel, and I jump up instantly to grab my woman in my arms, I just needed to feel her to ground me.

"Thank you, Mr. Scales." I shake my lawyers hand as we make it to the hallway.

"You son of a bit-." Mrs. Murphy comes lunging at us but more than likely aiming for my wife and before I can even react my mother draws her hand back, quickly coming forward, connecting with her face so hard she falls on the floor sliding maybe a foot or two away. This time we don't even bother after the judges decision, I walk hand in hand with my wife to the elevators with my parents trailing close behind us. We hear her arguing with her lawyer as we wait for it to open, and we hop on the moment it does.

"I am so glad that part Is all over." Sapphire expresses rubbing her shoulder against my arm and my mother as well as father agree with her. I am too far in my head in planning what to do with her old ass after a couple of months, I know my wife will want some parts so I might as well get out of my head and we can plan that later. We enjoy a nice quiet lunch eating some southern soul food until my girl starts feeling bad, so we get on the road to my parents townhouse, where we are spending the night until our flight in the morning. The past week has gone on by smoothly. We spent the weekend with the kids going to game rooms, out to eat, and the movies one night since we leave for the next two weeks. Wifey could not make up her mind on tropical or somewhere else she's never been so we are spending a week in the Turks & Caicos then flying to Italy, my woman loves her some pasta so what better place to get some. After an almost four-hour flight we are landing in Turks then taking a quick ride to our resort.

"Oh my gosh babe this place is beautiful." She spins around looking at the floating bar in the hotel pool, but we keep walking because I bought one of the huts out on the water. We meet up with our private concierge then hop in the golf cart to ride the rest of the way. She gets so excited when we get inside the when she sees the glass floor towards the deck area that has stairs leading right into the crystal blue water. The bed is a California king, light cedar, four post bed with white sheer curtains tied to each post. There was half a kitchen to the left with a round breakfast table then to the right was the open shower and separate soaking tub that sits in front of a glass window that can be frosted with a flick of the switch. I have some serious plans to fuck my wife in every inch of this place including that glass part of the deck.

"Babeeee." She screams running towards me and I gladly open my arms for her to jump into them which she does.

"Well, I have another surprise for you." She looks at me skeptically since she doesn't like surprises for the most part.

"Don't give me that look woman. The surprise is this is a special resort for couples into BDSM. They have a club inside and –"Before I can finish the concierge is back with my personal requests. I walk over to the door with Sapphire's arms and legs still wrapped around me the concierge smiles when he notices after I open the door. I step out the way for him to place the large velvet box on our bed.

"I take It we are in for a fun week inside this beautiful hut."

"Good you don't want to visit the club either." I ask her as I walk us over to the bed and then I sit down with her on my lap.

"No, I don't want to share anything we do while here well unless someone see's us making love on the deck tonight or in that big ass tub. I can careless about anyone seeing us so no frosted glass needed."

"You keep talking like that, I will have you pressed up against that glass as I tear that fat pussy up. There's a vibrating butt plug I ordered among other fun things." I groan out leaning forward to bite on that sensitive part of her neck and she moans.

"Say less but fuck those toys tonight I just want all of you." She decides to lean back to raise her dress over her head then throws it to the floor, leaving her in nothing but these black lace boy shorts that I notice when she leans back further has the crotch cut out. I can't help but reach between us and rub two of my fingers through her already slick folds initiating a moan from her when I slide my fingers in and out of her a few times. I lean down to suck one of her nipples in my mouth biting down on it ever so slightly and she gushes around my fingers that are moving against her G spot.

"Fuc... fuck. All I ever need is you just you Haze." She moans out at she continues to cum all over my finger as I give her other breast some attention.

"And you will always have me in any way you want my Phire." I remove my fingers from her sopping wet pussy, licking her juices off my fingers, then pull her by the neck for a long heated kiss. Still making out I stand walking us to the bathroom then pressing the button outside the shower to get it started at the perfect temperature. Sitting her on the toilet to relieve herself while I strip then grab her favorite bath bubbles and soap from our bags. After a much needed shower getting clean, we sit enjoying the view before ordering room service from the app on my phone then I do exactly what I said I would and fucked her up against that glass. Pressing her face against the glass with her soapy tits pressed against it and her moans greeting the concierge at the door as he pushes the food cart into the room. We have had an exquisite dining experience and the sex, fuck the sex. She edged me the other night and when I finally came it was so euphoric, for a few moments I was lightheaded. We only have one more night, so we are just making sure we have the most important things put up first when my phone rings.

"Hey ma... ma calm down I don't understand what you're saying." I try to calm her down even though I'm now on high alert because my mom is not the panicking type.

"Son, shit I'm sorry but someone attempted to kidnap Harmony and shot Gemini. He is fine the ambulance patched him up but sent him to the hospital for x-rays." I had the phone on speaker sitting on the dresser so the what the fuck that was shouted from the bathroom was expected. She came racing into the room soon after.

"Where are the kids are they ok? Did they catch the assholes that tried to take my baby?" She rapid fires questions at him but my father, the epitome of calm, answers all our questions then we end the call after letting him know we will be on the next flight home.

"I bet any amount of money it was my bitch ass aunt. I told you we should have just ended her ass." She rushes to throw everything she finds in our suitcases.

"Hey come here Sapphire." I instruct her tapping my lap after taking a seat on the edge of the bed. She starts to protest but knows I'm not going to repeat myself. She sits on my lap facing me with her legs wrapped around my waist.

"Baby our girl is safe, your father is ok, and we are headed to the airport to handle said problem because I agree. I need your calm levelheaded side with this. No mistakes, in and out, we have a honeymoon to finish, understood?"

"Fine but I'm doing it." She pouts acting like the brat I love so.

"Whatever you want baby." She finishes packing while I get our flights rearranged, call for the concierge to get us, and our ride to and from the airport. I know my woman will not calm down until we lay eyes on our kids then deal with this decrepit possum face bitch. We head straight to my parents townhome

125

the moment our car arrives and when we get in the door the kids rush us talking all at once about how scary it was.

"One at a time. Harmony baby how are you feeling?" I question her as she tucks herself under my arm as we walk to the living room where our parents are sitting. She doesn't speak until we are sitting on the couch, and she's balled up in my lap while holding Sapphire's hand the whole time.

"It was scary. They pulled up out of nowhere. If it weren't for Granddad and Paw Paw they would have gotten me." She expresses with her head resting on my chest while Sapphire's head is on my right shoulder, Destiny is on my left rubbing her sister's back, and Dontrell is siting on the floor resting his head on Sapphire's knee. Even though this is a scary moment for our family, I am smiling on the inside at out closeness.

"I wouldn't let that happen sis, over my dead body." Dontrell protest from the floor and she let Sapphire's hand go long enough to fist bump him.

"Daddy, are you really, ok?" Sapphire asks her dad who is sitting across from us in his Lazy boy with his arm in a sling with Mama Bentley sitting on the arm rubbing his bald head.

"It's going to take more then a little bullet to the arm to take ya old man out, so don't worry, ya mother is doing that enough." He jokes but I can tell he's doing good with his relaxed posture. I feel her looking up at me and I know I will be rescheduling that flight to Paris further out then a week later. I lean over and kiss her forehead earning me a smile. We sit and talk with our parents until we notice the kids falling off to sleep in their respective spots. Dontrell proclaimed himself to be a big boy, so he didn't need to be taken to bed so we carried the girls and made sure they were all tucked in nice. Once we get back downstairs, I give my wife the nod, but Our parents stand and tell me to come sit.

"Listen we know what you two are going to get into and we just want you both to be safe." My mom explains and they all nod.

"I want you to make sure that bitch is finally dead, sister or not nobody fucks with my kids." Mama Bentley snaps.

"I already know Pops; on my life she will be good." I reassure Pops Bentley who is giving me a look that says all I need to know. We head to a storage unit an old army buddy keeps at this old storage place in the booney's with two old school cars which is perfect for tonight. We walk over to the one I am keeping until our home is built.

"Babe, I hope all this will be moved to a secure room at home once it's done. I don't need anyone finding this." She asks as she runs her hands over my knife collection while I grab a few needles filled with some concoctions that will give my woman the satisfaction she needs.

"You already know me baby, now let's get this over with I need to get in those guts again before we go be with our babies." I inform her while rubbing on her plump apple bottom.

"Yes sir." She leans back for a kiss and I plant a quick one then smack her on the ass. Throwing my duffel bag in the backseat after making sure wifey is securely fastened in we head off.

Chapter Eleven

Sapphire Jenkins

The ride to my aunt's is spent with Haze rubbing circles on my thigh and me doing the same on his forearm as I look out the window. I don't know how he found it but of course my husband did find the trail in the woods that leads to her back yard.

"Hey babe looks like we are going to be making more than one stop tonight. She used two of my dumb ass cousins to try and take our baby." I fill him in on the text that just came through the burner we picked up at the storage unit since we left our phones at his parents. I'm still sitting in the car while he changes.

"Bet, I have a few other toys." He grabs his duffel bag and squats in front of me to make me hop on his back. At first, I wanted to be a brat about it but thought this wasn't the time and just hopped on. He carried me the whole mile up the bumpy trail. We stopped less than a quarter mile away from the house for me to disable any cameras she had, which turned out to be none since Uncle Trenton has apparently stopped paying for all bills already so she can't afford much. I hand Haze back the tablet he gave me and we finish our walk right up to her back door. With just a few turns of the lock pic the lock clicks and we enter through the kitchen. After taking the back steps, we end up in front of the master bedroom door. We stood and listened for a few moments. She was clearly sleeping comfortably, either she didn't know they failed or felt so high and mighty that she thought everything was

Gucci. He walks over to the side of her bed while I stand at the foot.

"Wake up ya bottom feeding crotch sniffer." He taps her on the side of her with his gun and she snaps up eyes wide.

"Wha... what... what the hell are you heathens doing in my home? Get out before I call the cops." She tries to get brave which earns her Haze's Glock seventeen pressed to the center of her forehead.

"Now I usually don't like to commit violence against women but my beautiful wife has no problem so we can either do this bloody or minimum damage you choose."

"You –"She starts to get smart but then thinks twice of it. Haze moves from her side of the bed and starts taking plastic out then laying it on the floor then reaches back in for three long needles each filled with different color liquids. I see the moment just how much danger she is in registers in her eyes, but she doesn't bother to scream seeing as she decided she wanted to act like she was better than everyone and had Uncle Trenton build her this large house further down from the rest of the family.

"Not so brave now, are you? I can't believe you thought it was a good idea to try and take my damn child then use our fucking family to do it. Like really how stupid can you be." She knows I don't need an answer, so she just lowers her head.

"Hmm I really thought she would have more fight in her, maybe those bitch ass cousins of yours will be more fun." Haze walks up placing his arm around my waist then turns my head towards his for a heated kiss then points towards the needles he laid out at the foot of the king size bed.

"Well *aunty* what color would you like to try?" I inquire as she looks at me with tears in her eyes.

"Sapphire I am sorry for all the trouble I caused; I was just so mad and wanted my granddaughter to be with me. Let me live and I promise I will not bother you guys ever again." She attempts to plead for her life but that shit falls on deaf ears.

"Well babe you know I love me some red and purple. Hmm *inny minnie miny mo which color do I choose?"* I sing out loud clearly, scaring the shit out of her further because next thing know I smell piss.

"Damn you mummified looking bitch I know you are old and all, but you can control your bladder." Haze and I both tune our face up as her piss smells like a gallon of ammonia.

"Get the fuck up wit ya nasty ass." I walk her to the bathroom to clean up as Haze strips the bed spraying it with some type of mixture that starts to clear up the smell then puts new linens down. After she changes, I push her down onto the chair in the middle of the plastic and quickly jab the needle into her thigh pushing the purple liquid into her then standing back while Haze wraps her with this wide band satin like restraint.

"I never even asked, what does it do?" I look up at him as he walks behind me and wraps his arms around me.

"The purple makes her bleed from the eyes and ears then all her organs start to shut down. Heart attack is what it will all look like in the end when they find her." He explains leaning down to bite on that sensitive part of my neck I love so much and I moan.

"Babe, you keep that up I will fuck you right here." I moan as he continues to kiss up my neck.

"Pull those shorts down, get on your knees and put the ass in the air how I like." He demands smacking my ass through my shorts and I do as he tells me. I look over at my aunt and she looks like a deer caught in headlights then blood starts leaking from the side. I feel the heat radiating off Haze as he positions himself behind me. He runs his fingers through my wet pussy, and I push against them trying to get the pressure I need. This man has me so turned on its borderline insane.

"Always so wet and needy for me." He moans sucking my juices from his fingers then slamming into me all the way to the hilt.

"Oooooh fuck baby just like that." I moan as he gives me the quickest deep strokes that steal my damn breath.

"Breath baby, you taking this dick so good." He directs me while wrapping my ponytail around his hand. I'm so enthralled with my husband fucking the shit out me initiating streams of cum from my pussy I forgot that stupid bitch was over there dying and from the looks of it she was just about gone. Seeing the life leave her eyes made me cream all over my man's dick.

"That's my wife give me all that nut, every fucking drop." He grunts lifting one of his legs to plant his foot flat on the floor while still kneeling on the other making him hit my pussy at a different angle and all I can do is exactly what he told me.

"I feel that shit Haze, cum in ya pussy baby."

"Ugghhh fuck woman. I can't wait till I can cum in this pussy and you give me a baby." He grunts while emptying streams of his cum into me and I cum again with him. We clean ourselves up, cleaning up the blood from the dead bitch before laying her in the bed like she is peacefully sleeping then head out the same way we came in. Once at the car I check my text and we have the location of the two dummies she used. Turns out she persuaded those fools into grabbing Harmony by saying she had evidence we conspired to kill Monique all along and were mentally abusing Harmony. I decided it was enough killing of family tonight and instead had Haze give them some concoction that would make them forget the last few days or so. On our drive back to his parents from the storage place I get a taste for my lollipop, so I lean over the center console and pull him out. I wet him up really good and take him right to the back of my throat then swallow.

"Fuuckk damn baby swallow yo shit." He moans and I do.

THE END

EPIOLUGE

TWO YEARS LATER

Well clearly that fertile ass man of mines did not need to have his vasectomy reversed because two months after our honeymoon in Turks I was getting pregnant on four different pregnancy tests. I really thought I would want to stay working but when I tried going back after my maternity leave all I wanted to do was go back home to my family and our mini farm. So yes, your girl is now a stay at home wife. I will, however, be doing farmers markets next month with my sister in laws to sell and give away some of the produce have been growing. The whole family ended up moving to Houston once they found out I was pregnant. Garnet sold part of his land to Jr so we all could be close to each other while mama and papa Jenkins took over the house my brother purchased next to my parents. We named our son Zeke Haze Jenkins and he is one hyper baby going on two years old. Harmony is eighteen now and thriving at TSU as a Computer Engineering student. We had therapy lined up for her after her grandmother's body was discovered but the girl didn't even shed a tear, nor did she want to go to the funeral. We left it at that after about three sessions and the therapist stating she seemed to be ok but revealed that her mother only treated her nicely when Haze was around, and her grandmother treated her like some type of trophy instead of family. That made me wish I could resurrect their asses and then kill them all over again, but she is good now is what I keep telling myself. Dontrell has taken up boxing with his dad and uncles, he has been having a bit of a protector's complex since the incident with Harmony.

Thankfully my wonderful husband has been on daddy duty with all the kids real heavy. Destiny has taken up cheerleading and loving every girly moment of it. I have never seen so many damn ribbons and tennis skirts in my life. She has also signed up for gymnastics which made perfect sense for my perfectionist. She is at the top of the cheerleading pyramid and has been pushing herself to land her flips off the top. Now as far as that hunk of a husband of mines he is right here in the yard building my latest raised plant bed after putting up the new rain barrels while I rock in my chair rubbing my protruding belly since this man has knocked me up again. He stayed at home helping take care of everything the first year then started a construction company with our brothers and dads. I never felt so loved on. He planned a babymoon when I was eight months to this maternity spa in the mountains of New Mexico since we didn't want to be too far from the family. It was December so thankfully it wasn't too hot. If I wasn't already pregnant I sure as hell would have been with all the sex we had. It was perfect.

HAZE

Being married to my soul in human form has been the most peaceful and loving two years of my life. She has me out here building another one of her raised plant beds, who am I kidding she didn't even ask she just said out loud the other day in the garden she wanted another one for more collard greens. That woman doesn't have to ask me for a damn thing ever. I'm still in awe the way she carried my first-born boy and is carrying our daughter this time around. We decided she would be the last child she would get pregnant with at least but we still may adopt or foster, apparently, it's something she has always wanted to do and I'm down. I have an appointment next week to see what happened with my damn vasectomy because I will not let my woman go through all that pain to get tubes removed or have a full hysterectomy if she doesn't want or need to have it done. I am glad my brothers and I along with our dads started the construction company though after building our over six thousand square foot family home, it gave us all something else to do together plus I like working with my hands. Come to think about it I know something I can do with my hands right now since I'm done with this raised bed. My wife clearly is reading my mind because she gives me the side eye when getting up from her rocking chair on the back porch swaying that juicy ass of hers in that sundress I love. Life is finally good and I will continue to do everything to keep it this way. Oh, and don't worry we cleared out the lake, my baby came up with a new way to dispose of family traitors, but if I told you I'd have to kill you too.

About The Author

Lala B.

Hey y'all! I'm Lala B., a 35-year-old mama of two and a recent country girl transplant. I've been writing for pleasure since I was a kid, and in February 2025, I finally published my first book—dream come true! With a background in tech and a wild imagination, I pour my heart into every page. I love thrillers, romantasy, dark romance, urban romance, and sooo much more. If it's bold, emotional, and a little messy—I'm all in. Welcome to my world!

Find Me On Social Media:

Facebook- https://facebook.com/authorlalab

Facebook Group: https://www.facebook.com/share/g/15GNVHNitN/

Instagram: https://instagram.com/authorlalab

Tiktok: https://tiktok.com/authorlalab

Books By This Author

Love Unconventional: The Fredericks Family
Series